"Chris, are you thinking what I'm thinking?" Susan asked.

"I am if what you're thinking is that this isn't a hoax, but that Natasha is serious. *Very* serious."

Susan nodded. "And I'll tell you something else I'm thinking. You and I may have played our share of pranks, and sometimes we've even managed to help people out. But I think you've got to agree with me when I say that this time, we're dealing with something that's over our heads."

"*Way* over our heads!"

Also by Cynthia Blair:

Young Adult Novels
Published by Fawcett Juniper Books:

THE BANANA SPLIT AFFAIR

THE HOT FUDGE SUNDAY AFFAIR

STRAWBERRY SUMMER

THE PUMPKIN PRINCIPLE

STARSTRUCK

MARSHMALLOW MASQUERADE

FREEDOM TO DREAM

THE CANDY CANE CAPER

Adult Romances

LOVER'S CHOICE*

BEAUTIFUL DREAMER

COMMITMENT

JUST MARRIED

ALL OUR SECRETS

*Also published by Fawcett Books

THE PINK LEMONADE CHARADE

Cynthia Blair

FAWCETT JUNIPER • NEW YORK

RLI: $\frac{\text{VL 5 \& up}}{\text{IL 6 \& up}}$

A Fawcett Juniper Book
Published by Ballantine Books

Library of Congress Catalog Card Number: 88-91024

ISBN 0-449-70258-8

Manufactured in the United States of America

First Edition: June 1988

One

"Christine, for the third *time, what well-known English* author wrote *Pride and Prejudice*?"

Christine Pratt snapped out of her daydreaming as she suddenly realized that someone was talking to her. She blinked, looked around for a few seconds, and then remembered that she was sitting in school, in the middle of her second period English class. But instead of listening to Mr. Collins's lecture on English literature of the nineteenth century, she had been a million miles away. And as if that weren't already bad enough, she'd just gotten caught.

"Sorry, Mr. Collins." Chris gulped. "I guess I wasn't really paying attention."

"Christine, saying that you weren't paying attention is quite an understatement. It's like saying that Romeo and Juliet had a little crush on each other!"

The class broke into laughter, and Chris could feel her cheeks turning pink.

"Jane Austen wrote *Pride and Prejudice*," a familiar voice, a few seats back, piped up.

Chris turned around and smiled gratefully at Holly Anderson, her best friend.

"That's right, Holly," said Mr. Collins. "Thank you. And I'm sure that Chris owes you her gratitude, as well, for bailing her out of that one."

When the bell rang a few seconds later, signifying the end of second period, Chris Pratt heaved a sigh of relief. She immediately gathered up her books, cast a woeful look at Mr. Collins, and headed toward the door of the classroom along with the rest of the students.

"We're starting *Tale of Two Cities* in class tomorrow, Christine," Mr. Collins called after her. "Make sure you read the first three chapters tonight, so you'll be ready for the class discussion. And please make sure you get a good night's sleep! At home, I might add—not in my classroom!"

"Gee, Chris," said Holly as the two girls strolled toward third period history, another class they took together. "Not paying attention in class isn't at all like you."

"I know, Holly." Chris sighed. "It's just that lately, all I can think about is that in just a few short months, we'll all be graduating!"

"I can't wait, either," Holly commented wistfully. "It's pretty exciting, isn't it? Just think: We'll all be moving on to brand-new adventures, going on to college or getting our first full-time jobs."

"But that's the problem!" Chris wailed. "*I* still haven't figured out what I want to *do* after graduation! Sure, I've applied to colleges, but I'm not sure whether I really want to go or not. After all, I still haven't decided what I want to be when I grow up!"

It was true; that very subject had been occupying Chris's thoughts more and more lately. Now that she was a senior at Whittington High School, everyone she knew was busy making plans for their futures. Sometimes it seemed as if she were the only one who hadn't yet chosen one clear-cut direction.

"You know who's really got it made?" Chris went on mournfully.

"Who?"

"My twin sister, Susan. That's who."

Holly thought for a few seconds. "Well, Chris, it's true that ever since she was a little girl, she's wanted to study at an art school, and then go on to have a career as an artist. But look at everything *you've* got going for yourself!"

Chris eyed her friend skeptically as the two girls inched along the crowded corridors of Whittington High. "Like what?"

"Well, like the fact that you're outgoing, and friendly, and—and you're never at a loss for something to say. Why, you can talk yourself out of just about *any* situation!"

Chris couldn't help laughing at Holly's summation of her special skills. After all, it happened to be right on the nose. "Maybe, but what good is any of that in helping me decide what to *do* with the rest of my life?"

"Well, if it's any consolation, Chris, I'm not sure exactly what I want to do after college, either." Holly shrugged. "But the way I look at it, lots of people go to college without knowing what they want to do with their education—or even what they want to study, for that matter. But they take all kinds of different courses, and, sooner or later, they find something they're interested in.

"To be perfectly honest, Chris, I have absolutely no doubt that that's going to happen to you," Holly went on encouragingly. "And I'm sure that as soon as that happens, watch out! You and I have been friends long enough for me to know that once you find something that's important to you, you jump into it, head first."

"I suppose you're right."

Despite her reluctant agreement, however, Chris wasn't convinced. She kept wishing that something—*anything*—would happen that would help her decide where she was heading. Then, perhaps, she'd be able to muster up some enthusiasm for starting college in the fall.

But Chris didn't have much of a chance to ruminate about her future as she and Holly continued walking through the corridor. All of a sudden, she felt herself nearly toppling over as someone fell against her, pushing her so hard that she gasped. In fact, she was so surprised by the sudden impact that she threw her arms up into the air, letting go of all her schoolbooks. They fell to the floor with a loud bang, and then, before she even knew what had happened, she saw that her textbooks, her notebooks, several pens, and half a dozen loose pieces of paper were scattered at her feet, all over the floor.

"What on *earth*! . . ." She whirled around and found herself face-to-face with Skip Desmond, a boy she had never really taken the time to get to know, but who lately seemed to be making a point of being a nuisance whenever he was around her. "Skip, what do you think you're *doing*?"

Skip was wearing a huge grin, looking as if he

couldn't have cared less about what he had just done. In fact, from the belligerent tilt of his chin, it was fairly obvious that knocking into Chris had been no accident.

"Sorry about that," he said coolly, still grinning in that annoying way. He wasn't a bad-looking boy, with his light brown hair and blue eyes, but the way he was acting lately made it hard for him to seem attractive to anybody. "Guess I didn't notice you, Chris. But now that I have . . ." He came over to her and put his arm around her shoulders. "How about you and me getting together after school later on? You know, I've been meaning to ask you out for a long time now. . . ."

"Take your hands off me!" Chris demanded. "And I'd sooner go out with—with Mr. *Collins* than you, Skip Desmond!"

Instead of being offended, the arrogant boy just laughed.

"Your loss, Miss High and Mighty," he replied, and he sauntered off, still grinning as if he had just said the most clever thing in the world.

"Ooh, that Skip Desmond gets me so mad." Chris was seething as she watched him walk away. She leaned over and retrieved all her belongings. "He's such a . . . such a—"

"Oh, come on, Chris," said Holly. "Don't be so hard on him. He's just showing off, that's all. I hear his parents aren't getting along too well these days, and that he's having some problems because of it."

"Hmmm, that's too bad. I hadn't heard about that." Chris sighed. "Even so, what does he have to pick on *me* for?"

Holly chuckled, amused that the answer to that question wasn't obvious to Chris. "Because he *likes* you, silly! Only Skip is the kind of boy who doesn't know how to show it. You know, the type who feels uncomfortable letting people know how he really feels. So instead, he . . . well, he does dumb things like knock your books all over the floor."

"Well, I just wish he'd find somebody else to concentrate his energies on, well-meaning or otherwise," Chris grumbled as the two girls started on their way once again. She refused to let Skip's immaturity get her down for very long, however. "Now, where were we? Ah, yes; we were talking about the reason why I've been having such a hard time listening in class lately."

"Actually, Chris," Holly said with a teasing grin, glad that her friend was willing to forget about the unpleasant incident that had just occurred, "in case you haven't noticed, you're not the only one who's been having a hard time paying attention in class lately. I have, too—but for an entirely different reason."

"Really?" Chris blinked. "What's that?"

"All of a sudden, I've got a terrible case of spring fever! You know, it isn't easy, sitting in a classroom all day, while outside the sun is shining, flowers are starting to poke their pretty little heads out, and the air has that special freshness to it."

Even though she was in such a pensive mood, Chris had to agree. She smiled ruefully. "Now that you mention it, I've been noticing that this change in seasons has been having an effect on me, too."

"And knowing that spring vacation is only a few weeks away doesn't help, either," Holly went on. "Just think: a whole week off. No school, no homework . . . and no sitting in classrooms! I can hardly wait!" She glanced over at her friend. "Made any plans yet, Chris?"

"No, not yet. But one thing's for sure." Chris hugged her schoolbooks tightly against her chest as she and Holly continued to make their way down the corridor. "I would *love* to do something different—to take my mind off things, if nothing else. I'd love to do something I've never done before. Something wonderful and exciting and maybe even a little bit daring."

"Uh-oh, Chris," a teasing voice from out of nowhere suddenly interjected. "What are you up to *now*?"

She whirled around and found herself face to face with her twin sister, Susan.

"Caught me." Chris chuckled. "Hi, Sooz. Actually, I wasn't planning anything. I was just . . . dreaming. Holly and I were talking about the fact that spring vacation is only a few weeks away now."

"And your sister and I already have a bad case of spring fever," Holly informed her with a grin, flicking a strand of her long blond hair over her shoulder.

"Right," Chris agreed. Already she had forgotten her worries about her future, at least for the moment. After all, it was so much more pleasant to concentrate on the arrival of such an exhilarating new season. "And I was just saying that I'm really in the mood to do something *different*."

"Now *that's* what I call a coincidence!" said Susan. "Or at least good timing."

"Really? Why? What on earth are you talking about, Sooz?"

Susan Pratt just smiled mysteriously.

"Not to change the subject or anything," she went on, "but have you had history yet?"

"Nope. Holly and I have it now. Ms. Parker's third period class. Why, have you?" Chris was puzzled.

"Why, yes, as a matter of fact. I have it second period. I just got out."

Chris peered at her twin for a few seconds, then exploded. "Susan Pratt, you're hiding something! What is it? What happened in your history class today? And whatever it is, is it going to happen in mine, too?"

But Susan refused to say a word. She just continued smiling that same impish smile.

"Soo-oo-ooz! . . ."

Just then the bell rang. The few students who were still lingering in the halls of Whittington High School scurried off to their third period classes. Within a few seconds the corridors were empty.

"Let me just tell you one thing," Susan finally said, still smiling mischievously. "Christine Pratt, you're in for a *big* surprise!"

"What kind of surprise?" Chris called after her. "A *good* surprise? Is it something I'll like?"

But her twin had already vanished, dashing into a classroom nearby for her math class.

"Honestly, that sister of mine!" Chris pretended to complain to Holly as the two of them stepped into Ms. Parker's classroom, right across the hall. "Sometimes she drives me *bananas*!"

But Holly knew only too well that the Pratt twins were as close as any two sisters could possibly be. And the fact that they were identical seventeen-year-olds, with the same short chestnut brown hair, alert brown eyes, high cheekbones, and pert ski-jump noses, actually had very little to do with it.

As a matter of fact, the two girls were really quite

different. Chris was the outgoing twin. She was active in school sports and clubs, she spent endless hours talking on the phone and planning her busy social life, and she went out every chance she got. Susan, on the other hand, was quiet and shy. She loved reading, playing with the girls' pet cat, Jonathan, and, most of all, painting. It was true that she planned to go to art school after high school graduation, so that, one day, she could be a professional artist.

No, what really made the Pratt twins such good friends was their shared love of adventure, and their love of playing tricks and practical jokes. And although they were only seniors in high school, the two girls already had quite a history of doing just that.

It had all started with *The Banana Split Affair*, when Chris and Susan traded identities for two weeks so that each could learn more about what the other's life was like. Since then, they had gone on to take advantage of their similar appearances many times.

They'd helped a family who was on the verge of being forced to sell the summer camp that had been in their family for years, done some sleuthing that helped keep a children's hospital from having to close down . . . Chris had even pretended to be a boy for a week so that she and her girlfriends could find out more about what made the opposite sex tick. Every time they played one of their pranks, they also helped someone out, even as they had a good time and learned some valuable lessons themselves.

But there was no time for thinking about the fun the two girls had had together in the past. Not now, when history class was about to begin. Besides, Chris was already too wrapped up in wondering what Susan had been talking about to think about anything else.

Ms. Parker, however, had other plans for third period. As soon as the class quieted down, she launched into a lecture on the causes of World War I. Once again, Chris was finding it hard to concentrate. Perhaps her sister had just been teasing her. Maybe there wasn't really any "surprise" after all. . . .

She tore a blank piece of paper out of her spiral notebook, jotted down a note that read, "Holly, What on earth do you think Susan was talking about before?" and folded it up as small as she could. Then she turned around in a way that she hoped looked casual, passed the note to Holly, and turned around to face the front again—only to find herself nose-to-nose with Ms. Parker.

"Christine, is it possible that you're actually *bored* by World War I—even though it was the biggest war the world had ever seen before in its entire history?"

"I'm really sorry, Ms. Parker," said Chris. "It's just that I'm finding it so hard to concentrate today!"

Holly immediately jumped in, anxious to help out her friend once again. "I can't concentrate either, Ms. Parker! I've got an awful case of spring fever. I think we *all* have, Chris and me and everybody else."

"That's right," Chris agreed. "Just look outside the windows! The sun is shining, the flowers are starting to bloom . . ."

Instead of being angry, Ms. Parker laughed. "You've got a point there, girls. March isn't exactly the easiest time of the year to sit in a classroom. It may surprise you to know that teachers get spring fever, too!"

She walked up to the front of the classroom again.

"Well, I'd been planning to wait until the end of the period to make this announcement, but I might as well tell you all about it now." With a twinkle in her eye, she added, "After all, I have a feeling that Chris and Holly and I aren't the *only* ones in here who've got a bad case of spring fever!"

Chris sat up straight in her chair, anxious to hear Ms. Parker's announcement—no doubt the surprise that her twin sister had been teasing her about. She glanced over at Holly and saw that she, too, was listening intently.

"I'm sure you're all aware that spring vacation is only a few weeks away," Ms. Parker began. "This year, for the first time in Whittington High's history, we're planning a school trip, open to juniors and seniors."

"Where to?" asked one of the senior girls, sitting in front. Chris just held her breath.

"Washington, D.C."

The entire class broke into excited chatter. Washington, D.C.! Chris could hardly believe her ears. That *was* exciting news! It sounded like exactly what she needed. And from the way Susan had been talking, it sounded as if she was already planning to go.

Better double that reservation, Chris thought with a grin.

The class finally quieted down, and Ms. Parker continued. "We'll be flying into Dulles Airport on Wednesday night, right in the middle of the week of your spring break. And we'll be coming back late Sunday morning. That means you'll have all day Thursday, Friday, and Saturday for sightseeing."

"Oh, boy!" cried Timothy Patterson, a sandy-haired senior boy, and, Chris knew, her sister's current crush.

"We'll be able to see the Lincoln Memorial, and the White House, and the Capitol. . . ."

"Don't forget the Vietnam War Memorial!" someone else piped up.

"And the Smithsonian Institution's museums," said another student. "I understand there's an art museum, and a space museum, and an American history museum. . . . Wow! I can hardly wait!"

"I know; it's all very exciting," Ms. Parker said, holding up her hands for silence. "But there's even *more*." She paused for a moment, as if wanting to add dramatic impact to what she was about to say. "Whittington High has been invited to participate in a special cultural exchange program while we're in Washington."

"'A cultural exchange program'?" repeated Tim Patterson. "What's that?"

Holly Anderson answered that question for him. "It means that while we're in Washington, we'll get to meet some students from another country."

"That's right, Holly," Ms. Parker said. "During our stay, we'll be getting to know some of the younger members of a ballet company, young men and women who are about your age. The ballet troupe is coming over from Moscow for its very first visit to the United States."

"Moscow!" Chris cried. "We're going to meet some Russian dancers? Oh, boy!"

"As a matter of fact, we'll be doing a bit more than just meeting them," Ms. Parker went on to explain. "They've invited us to watch one of their dance classes. In turn, we've invited them to a little party, on Saturday night.

"And then, as if all that weren't already thrilling

enough, we'll be their special guests at their premier performance. It's their very first American appearance, and it's being held at the Kennedy Center."

Cries of "Wow!" and "Oh, boy!" rose up all around the classroom. Chris was already in seventh heaven, daydreaming about her upcoming trip to Washington. This was exactly the kind of thing she had been wishing for!

"*Now* how's your spring fever, Holly and Chris?" teased Ms. Parker. She had already begun passing out permission slips, along with a sheet of paper printed with all the details of the upcoming school trip.

"Gee, Ms. Parker," Chris returned with a chuckle. "I'd say our spring fever is suddenly turning into an epidemic!"

By lunchtime, the trip to Washington, D.C., and the school's cultural exchange with the younger members of the Russian ballet troupe, was already all that anyone was talking about.

"You're going, aren't you?" Holly asked Chris over tuna fish sandwiches. The two of them had just sat down in the school cafeteria and were having lunch with Susan and her best friend, Beth Thompson.

"Are you kidding?" Chris replied enthusiastically. "I wouldn't miss this trip for the world!"

"Me, either," Susan agreed. She turned to the pretty, soft-spoken girl with dark curly hair who was sitting beside her. "How about you, Beth? You've already signed up for the trip, haven't you?"

Beth nodded. "I sure have! My name's practically the first one on the list!"

"We're going to have so much fun," said Chris. "Just

think: the four of us, running around Washington, D.C., having the time of our lives. . . ."

"The four of you?" a male voice echoed. "Does that mean there's no room for me, Chris?"

She turned around and saw Gary Graham, wearing a huge grin. He had just been strolling by, his lunch tray in hand. Gary was a good-looking senior with dark hair, hazel eyes, and an easygoing manner that was reflected in his readiness to smile. Actually, she didn't know him very well, but lately getting to know him better had become a very high priority.

"Hi, Gary. Don't tell me you're planning to come along on the Washington trip, too!"

"Okay, then I won't tell you," Gary joked. "But if you happen to see somebody at the Natural History Museum who looks a lot like me—except that he's wearing sunglasses and carrying a big guidebook—don't be surprised!"

"Gee, this trip is sounding better and better every minute!" Chris exclaimed. "I have a feeling that our little jaunt to Washington, D.C., may well turn out to be the most exciting thing that's ever happened to me!"

As she took a big bite of her tuna fish sandwich, Chris had absolutely no idea how true her prediction would turn out to be—and that the word *exciting* would prove to be nothing less than the understatement of the century.

Two

"I can't believe we're really here!" breathed Chris, stepping off the 727 that had just landed at Dulles, Washington's large international airport. "Just think, Sooz: Just a few hours ago, we had lunch in Whittington. Yet now here we are, in time for dinner, hundreds of miles away!"

"And in our nation's capital, no less!" Susan added, with just as much enthusiasm. "Boy, I'm *thrilled* to be here!"

Susan Pratt was more than ready for her tour of Washington, D.C., to get started. And even though the group's sightseeing excursions wouldn't really get rolling until the following morning, she was already dressed for exploring a brand-new city on foot: low-heeled walking shoes, a neat yet comfortable skirt and blouse, a lightweight sweater in case this warm Wednesday evening in April turned cool, and, of course, a camera, hanging around her neck on a black nylon strap.

Her twin sister, walking next to her, was also prepared—in her own way. She was wearing a pair of mint green jeans, a green-and-white-striped cotton sweater, and her favorite vacation footwear: a pair of running shoes. The only thing that gave away the fact that she, too, was a tourist was the small brown suitcase that she was swinging alongside her as she walked.

"I wonder if we'll see anyone we recognize at the airport," Chris mused. "You know, senators, congressmen, presidents . . ."

Susan laughed. "You have quite an imagination, Chris. Well, maybe we won't see anybody like that here at the airport, but don't forget that, according to our schedule, we'll be sitting in on a session of Congress tomorrow morning, right after our bus tour. We'll see plenty of faces that we recognize from the newspaper and television there. I can hardly wait!"

"That will be pretty exciting," Chris agreed. "I'm really looking forward to that—and about a million other things. But at the risk of sounding like some boring tourist, I must admit that my main concern right now is getting something cold to drink. I'm positively *dying* of thirst!"

"I read somewhere that airplane travel often has that effect on people," commented Beth, who had just joined the twins in the waiting area. It was right outside the gate through which they'd just entered the interior of the airport. "But I'm afraid you'll just have to wait a while, Chris. Ms. Parker and the other chaperones made us all swear on our lives that we'd wait right here, so they could keep the group together until they take attendance. Better not go wandering off. Don't worry, though; I'm sure we'll be out of here and on our way to the hotel soon enough. You can get something to drink there."

Just then, Holly Anderson wandered over. She was dressed very much like her best friend Chris, but wore her long blond hair pulled back in a ponytail for a change.

"Hey, guess what," she said. "I just heard an announcement over the loudspeaker. A flight from Moscow just landed, somewhere over at the other end of the terminal. Wouldn't it be funny if it turned out those Russian ballet dancers we're supposed to meet while we're here were on the flight?"

"It sure would," Susan agreed. "I'm really looking forward to that part of the trip. Gee, I've never even been to a ballet class, much less to one where the students are real Russian ballet stars! Don't you think that'll be fun, Chris?"

But Chris hardly heard what her sister had just said. She was craning her neck, trying to see what was beyond their waiting area, which was roped off from the rest of the terminal. The waiting area was already filling up with Whittington High School students; even so, she suspected that it would be some time yet before they finally got to their hotel. And she truly was thirsty.

"Listen, we've still got a few more minutes before Ms. Parker and the other chaperones take attendance," she told her friends. "I'm going to sneak out of here and find a refreshment stand."

"Chris . . . ," her sister warned.

"It'll only take a minute. They'll never miss me. Besides," she added with a mischievous grin, "if they start roll call before I get back, you can always pretend you're me!"

"What about the fact that you and I don't even look like sisters right now, much less twins?" Susan protested.

It was true; when the Pratt girls dressed in the ways that made each of them feel most comfortable, they didn't look at all alike—unless, of course, someone really took the time to study their faces.

"Wing it!" Chris had already taken off, her small brown suitcase still in hand. She wasn't too concerned about being missed during roll call, since she knew she'd be back in only a few minutes.

Beyond the waiting area in which she and the other Whittington High School students had been waiting was a long, wide corridor, seemingly stretching on forever. Off it were waiting rooms that surrounded the gates leading to the planes themselves. Chris hurried through the corridor, clutching her suitcase.

Even in her rush, however, she managed to enjoy herself as she observed the other travelers. What a varied assortment of people there was gathered here. She marveled at the different languages she heard, some of which she couldn't even identify, and the various accents with which she heard English being spoken. Different faces, different colorings, different modes of dressing . . . it was truly exhilarating, seeing all the different designs that people came in! She was almost disappointed when she finally spotted a refreshment stand, since it marked the end of her little exploration.

She bought a glass of pink lemonade in a paper cup and immediately gulped down half of it. Then she noticed that right across from the refreshment stand was a souvenir shop. She wandered over to it, and as she sipped the rest of her cold drink, she studied a display of T-shirts printed across the front with "Washington, D.C." Just as she was trying to decide if she should dip into her souvenir fund and splurge on one for herself, her attention was diverted by a loud voice, right behind her.

"Nyet, Ivan. No! You must stay with the group! No one is to go wandering off alone!"

Chris recognized the accent as Russian. And the tone of voice of the man who was speaking made it clear that he was quite serious in his warning. Curious, she followed "Ivan" and the man who had been scolding him. She was surprised to discover that Ivan was tall and muscular. He looked as if he were about eighteen or twenty years old—certainly much too old to be bossed around in such a manner.

The two men went over to a waiting area that was very much like the one in which Chris's classmates were gathered, even as she was off on her own, exploring the airport. There was a group waiting here, as well, although it was considerably smaller. About twenty people, most of them young, sat in the waiting area, talking in groups of two and three. And, she noticed as she got closer, they were all talking in a language that sounded very much like Russian.

Suddenly Chris's brown eyes grew round.

Is it possible these are *our* Russians? she wondered. The ones that we Whittington High School students are going to meet while we're in Washington? Maybe Holly was right. . . .

Fascinated, Chris stood off to one side, close enough to overhear some of what was being said, yet not quite close enough to be noticed. In fact, she pretended to be standing there, waiting for someone as she sipped the rest of her lemonade. But she kept her ears tuned.

"We should be talking English," one of the young women suddenly said. "We need to practice."

Chris was startled to hear something she understood. Casually she moved over, until she was right behind the girl who had spoken, and set down her brown suitcase on the floor. She couldn't see the girl's face; in fact, she could only see her from the back. She had unusually broad shoulders, Chris noticed, and a tiny waist. Her long chestnut brown hair, similar in color to Chris's, was worn in a long thick braid, hanging down her back.

"Da, Natasha," the girl's friend replied. "We will talk in English." She, too, had long hair, but hers was blond and worn flowing and free. She was also slight of build, yet looked surprisingly athletic. "Are you frightened to be dancing *Coppelia* on Saturday night in front of American audience?"

"Oh, no," answered Natasha quickly. Then she laughed. "Maybe little bit frightened. . . ."

Chris could hardly believe what she was hearing. These *were* the dancers the Whittington High School students would be having their "cultural exchange" with; at least, that was how it seemed.

She looked at the two girls more carefully. She was trying to decide if they looked like dancers—without them noticing that she was staring at them, of course. They did look healthy and graceful and strong; she had noticed that right away. Even so, Chris couldn't be sure.

But what she heard next took away all her doubts.

"Well, Katya," said Natasha, "it will be fun to meet American students. I have never met any Americans. I do have relative who lives here, in New York, but I have never met her."

Wait until I tell Sooz! Chris thought gleefully. That thought reminded her that she had been away from the rest of her group much longer than she had intended. By now, Susan was probably getting nervous, if not downright angry.

Well, Chris thought ruefully, I guess I'll have plenty of time to find out more about Natasha and Katya and all the other Russian ballet dancers over the next few days. But for now, I'd better get back to where I'm supposed to be before someone misses me.

She was about to make her way back when she suddenly heard, over the airport's loudspeaker system, "Will passenger Christine Pratt please return to Gate Seventeen? Christine Pratt, please return to Gate Seventeen."

Uh-oh! she thought, suddenly in a panic. I've been caught!

Leaning over so quickly that she almost spilled what was left of her lemonade, she picked up the suitcase beside her. Then she started to hurry away, heading toward the airport's long corridor that would lead her back to her tour group. But before she had even had a chance to get six feet away, she felt someone grab her arm.

"Excuse me, miss," said a stern voice with a thick Russian accent, a voice that she recognized immediately. "I believe you are making a mistake."

"A mistake? What? I . . ."

Chris looked up and saw that, just as she'd suspected, her arm was being held by the same serious-looking man in the gray suit who, only a few minutes earlier, had been reprimanding the ballet dancer named Ivan.

"That suitcase you are holding. I believe it does not belong to you."

"But of *course* this is mine!"

Bewildered, Chris glanced down at the suitcase she had just picked up. Sure enough, it was hers. Or at least it *looked* just like hers. . . .

"Excuse me." This time, the voice she heard was much softer, and much more gentle. "But I think that is my suitcase." Natasha smiled at her sweetly. "You see, my suitcase looks very much like your suitcase. Look, mine is brown, yours is brown. I think you are in great hurry, and you took my suitcase instead of your own. It is what you call 'honest mistake,' no? It is accident."

Now Chris was beginning to understand. She studied more closely the suitcase in her hand. Sure enough; while it looked very much like hers, it wasn't. Sheepishly, she looked at the man, and then at Natasha.

"Gee, I'm really sorry. It was, as you said, just an 'honest mistake.'"

"Is no problem. It is easy to fix."

The two girls exchanged the suitcases they had each been holding. They also exchanged two shy smiles.

"Despite mistake, I am very pleased to make your acquaintance," Natasha said. "You are first American girl I have ever talked to."

"Really? Well, that's a real coincidence, since you happen to be the first Russian girl I've ever talked to!"

There were a million questions that Chris would have loved to ask, but the frowning man in the gray suit was still there, standing very close to Natasha, listening to every word they were saying to each other. Chris decided that letting on that she had been hanging around, listening in on their conversation—"spying," in a way—was not the best of ideas.

So instead, she said, "Are you visiting the United States for the first time?"

"Oh, yes!" Natasha was beaming. She was very pretty, Chris noticed, with large brown eyes, a small nose, and a big, friendly smile. "I have heard so much about your country, and I am looking forward to seeing it. And meeting people, too, of course. I have heard much about how nice people are here."

"Really? From whom?"

"I have relative—how you say, second cousin—who lives now in New York, and she writes me letters saying she has made many American friends here."

"No kidding!" Chris exclaimed. "What else did she tell you about the United States?"

The chaperone scowled, but Natasha didn't seem to notice. Instead, she was growing more and more excited.

"She tells me many things. All about television programs, and movie stars, and—how you say, video arcades—and *food*. Oh, yes, she tells me many things about food here."

Chris grinned. "Do you like to eat?"

"I *love* to eat. And I want to try everything while I am here. The Big Mac and the Whopper, and the ice cream sundae, and the pizza . . . oh, and one more thing she tells me about: the pink lemonade."

"Pink lemonade!" Chris looked at the paper cup she was still holding and laughed.

"Yes. They take lemonade—lemons and water and

sugar—but they make it *pink*! It sounds very pretty, and very good. You have heard of this pink lemonade?"

"I certainly have. I drink it all the time. As a matter of fact, I just drank an entire glass of it! See?"

"Ah, you are lucky, then. Not only do you have all these wonderful foods, but you can eat and drink all of them, any time you want. I do so love to eat, but I have to eat very little, so that *I* will stay very little. You see, I am a ballet dancer."

Chris pretended to be surprised. "Really? You're a dancer?"

"Yes. We are all dancers." Natasha opened her arms to signify the group of young people around her. "In fact, we are here in United States in order to perform. We dance *Coppelia* on Saturday night, at the Kennedy Center. You know this place?"

"Of course I know the Kennedy Center! As a matter of fact, it just so happens that I'm going to be in the audience this Saturday night. I'm a student at Whittington High School, and we're going to—"

"Whittington High School! I have heard of that place!" Excitedly, Natasha turned to the chaperone. "Mr. Pirov, that is school we are having cultural exchange program with, no?"

Mr. Pirov, the chaperone, simply answered, "Da." He still looked very unhappy.

"Then that means I will see you again soon," Natasha went on, wearing a broad smile. "My name is Natasha Samchenko. And your name?"

"Chris. Christine Pratt."

The two girls shook hands, both looking very pleased over their brand-new friendship.

"Listen, it was great talking to you, Natasha," Chris said, suddenly remembering that more than five minutes earlier, she had been paged over the airport's loudspeaker system—and that back at Gate Seventeen, Ms. Parker and the others were probably growing more annoyed, and perhaps even more worried, with each passing minute. "But I really have to run. I'm looking forward to seeing you again, though, and getting to know all your friends. Oh, and to seeing you dance, too."

Chris picked up her suitcase—the *right* suitcase, this time—and said a hasty good-bye. Then she dashed away, back to her group. Her cheeks were flushed as she took off. And it wasn't so much because she was in a hurry as because she was so excited.

Gee, just wait until I tell Sooz! she was thinking. Wait until I tell Holly and Beth and Ms. Parker . . . and everybody else, for that matter!

Meeting Natasha had made quite an impression on her, and she couldn't wait to share the news.

Chris was not the only one who was thinking about her meeting with the Russian ballet dancers as she hurried back to Gate Seventeen. The man in the gray suit, the dance troupe's chaperone, Mr. Pirov, was also thinking about it. Worrying about it, even. After all, it seemed like a very strange coincidence that this American girl Christine Pratt had almost the same suitcase as the ballet company's prima ballerina, and that she just "happened" to pick it up, supposedly by mistake. . . .

The more he thought about it, the more certain he became of one thing: He intended to keep a very close watch on this Christine Pratt over the next few days.

By the time Chris reached her group, she felt as if she were ready to burst.

"Guess what, Sooz!" she cried. "You'll never, *ever* guess what just happened to me!"

Immediately Chris began chattering away, telling Susan and Holly and Beth and everyone else nearby about her little adventure. As she did, she never dreamed that her innocent mistake was going to throw her into the most daring—and the most dangerous—escapade of her entire life.

Three

"Wake up, Beth!" cried Susan, shaking the shoulder of her sleepy roommate. "It's almost eight o'clock, and our tour bus leaves the hotel at nine sharp. Unless you want to spend our very first day in Washington sleeping, you'd better get a move on."

Slowly, reluctantly, a head of dark tousled hair emerged from underneath the covers. "Is it morning already?" Beth groaned.

"You bet. And we decided last night that we'd meet Chris and Holly at their room at eight-fifteen so we could all go down to the hotel coffee shop for breakfast together, remember?"

Susan was already up and raring to go, as she had been ever since seven o'clock. She had found it impossible to sleep when she was about to be set loose in Washington for the very first time, guidebook and camera and maps in hand.

The evening before, riding to the hotel from the

airport had given her and the other Whittington High School students their first glimpse of the city. Her appetite had really been whetted. The imposing monuments, the Washington Memorial and the Lincoln Memorial and the Jefferson Memorial, had been all lit up with white lights. The White House, with its manicured grounds, was stunning. The embassies, the government office buildings, the museums, the picturesque brownstones . . . each thing that their bus driver pointed out to his eager audience, sitting glued to the windows, had helped make what had only been a fantasy up until that moment suddenly become a reality.

And today she would have the chance to start exploring it all. She woke up early, immediately gave up on the idea of going back to sleep, and dressed in an outfit that was similar to what she'd worn the day before: a skirt and blouse, a pair of comfortable shoes, a sweater.

Perhaps it's not the most glamorous outfit in the world, thought Susan, glancing in the mirror as she pulled her dark brown hair off her face and fastened it on either side of her head with tortoiseshell barrettes. But at least it's the most *comfortable*. And after all, isn't that what being a tourist is all about?

Her twin, however, didn't happen to share her philosophy. When Susan and Beth knocked on the door of the double room across the hall from theirs, they were greeted by Chris—wearing electric pink pants and a bright orange shirt.

"Well, you certainly don't look very much like a tourist!" teased Susan.

"That's the idea," Chris returned with a grin. "But

just think how great these clothes will look when all the photographs come out!"

"What photographs?"

"Why, the ones you're going to take with that camera you've got hanging around your neck." Chris pretended to pose. "I'll be happy to be your model, any time you want!"

"You know what's really interesting?" Holly observed as she came out of the bathroom. "You two don't look anything at all like twins! I mean, even *knowing* that you're both identical makes it hard for me to see the resemblance right now."

Chris and Susan looked at each other and laughed.

"There's a good reason for that," Susan explained. "Even though Chris and I look the same on the outside, we're very different on the *inside*."

"That's right," her twin sister agreed. "And when each of us dresses the way we feel like dressing, that's bound to come out."

"Well, I think it's kind of eerie," Beth interjected. "Sometimes you two look so much alike that no one can tell you apart. Even your own parents! Or even us, your best friends. But other times, you both look so different that it's hard to believe that you're even sisters!"

"I guess that's just part of the fun of being identical twins," Chris said with a chuckle. "But I didn't come all the way to Washington to discuss being a twin. I came to do some sightseeing. Let's go!"

The rest of the morning was a whirlwind of activity. The twins and their friends boarded the tour bus promptly at nine and were treated to a ride around the city that helped get them oriented. It was fascinating, seeing some of the same sights they had seen the night before, only this time in broad daylight.

Washington was a beautiful city, planned in the late 1700's by Pierre Charles L'Enfant, a famous French city planner who designed the capital of the brand-new United States at George Washington's request. And that careful planning was reflected everywhere. Streets were wide and lined with trees, buildings were spaced far apart, and everywhere there was a feeling of openness—and freedom. Spring flowers had been planted in front of most of the buildings and many of the parks, and their vibrant colors added a certain vitality to the crisp lines of this elegant city.

After spending an hour observing the city from a tour bus, Chris and Susan were itching to get inside some of the buildings. Fortunately, their first stop was at the Capitol Building, where they sat in on a session of Congress. It was thrilling, sitting up in the balcony, listening as members of Congress from all over the country debated the pros and cons of a new bill that encouraged protection of the environment.

"I feel almost as if I'm watching history being made," Chris leaned over and whispered.

"You *are* watching history being made," her sister whispered back.

After lunch there was a tour of the White House. Susan was thrilled to see the bedroom in which Lincoln and Kennedy had slept. Chris, meanwhile, spotted a man ducking into one of the rooms that was off-limits to tourists and was convinced that she had seen the president.

When the tour was over, the students were given the rest of the day to explore the city on their own.

"Gee, we've already seen so much!" Chris exclaimed as she, her twin, and their best friends crossed the Mall, a long, wide strip of grassy park along which many major museums were lined up.

"Yes, but we've barely made a dent in the territory I hope to cover." Susan unfolded her map of the city. "Let's see, the Washington Mall. Oh, here it is. Wow, do you realize that there are *six* museums on this strip alone that I'd love to see? The American History Museum, the National Portrait Gallery—"

"Whoa—hold on!" Chris held up her hands dramatically. "Just *listening* to you rattle off that list is making my feet hurt!"

"I don't know about you," Holly interjected, "but I really want to see the Air and Space Museum. I belong to the science club at school, and we just did a huge project on space exploration for the county science fair. So that one's at the top of my list. Anybody care to join me?"

Chris seconded that motion heartily. "I would! I heard somebody on the bus say that you can actually go *inside* some of the spacecraft! They've got them all, too. Let's go there first."

Beth and Susan exchanged rueful glances.

"Somehow, that one wasn't on my list," said Susan.

"Me, either," Beth agreed.

"But I'll tell you what. Since we're all interested in seeing different things, how about if we split up? Chris, you and Holly can go over there to the Air and Space Museum." After glancing at her map one more time, Susan pointed to a huge modern building across the Mall.

"And we can start at the American History Museum, Susan," said Beth. "How does that sound?"

"Perfect!"

The two pairs split up, after agreeing to get together early that evening to share everything they had each seen and done on their own. Susan and Beth headed in one direction, and Holly and Chris went off in another.

"We're certainly managing to see a lot," Holly commented as she and Chris started across the Mall.

"I'll say!" Chris agreed. "Good thing I remembered to bring comfortable shoes!" Laughing, she pointed to her sneakers. "And it's also a good thing I practiced *walking* a lot before this trip. There's nothing worse than missing out on sightseeing because your feet hurt!"

As the two of them neared the Air and Space Museum and saw that beyond the dramatic glass wall that was its front there were suspended dozens of airplanes, rockets, and spaceships, they knew they were not about to be disappointed.

"Wow! Just *look* at this place!" Holly cried. "They've got every rocket ship I've ever heard of!"

"And they're not just replicas, either," Chris observed, glancing at one of the plaques hanging next to an old-fashioned glider. "These are the actual spaceships that people went up in. Gosh, what a collection!"

Something unusual caught her eye then, and she grabbed her friend's arm. "Ooh, look, Holly! There's a piece of the *moon*! Oh, let's go touch it. We'll probably never actually *get* there, but at least we'll always know that we came into contact with it once."

"So much for the romance of the moon." Holly smiled ruefully. "Next time I'm out with Hank, gazing up at the sky on a clear night, I'll be thinking about this dark, hard *rock* I'm touching. Those dreamy moonlit nights will never be quite the same again!"

The girls decided to start at the top of the museum, on the second floor, which was really more of a mezzanine. As they rode up the escalator, getting closer and closer to the huge spacecraft suspended from the ceiling, their eyes opened wide and their mouths dropped open.

"Hey, look!" Holly exclaimed, once they'd reached the second floor. "Here's one of those exhibits you were talking about. You can go right inside the lab where a whole bunch of astronauts lived for a few weeks, so they could see what it was like staying up in space for a long time. Let's start here, okay? Okay, Chris? *Chris!*"

She realized then that even though her friend was standing right next to her, she wasn't listening. Holly grabbed her arm.

"Christine Pratt, what on earth has come over you? All of a sudden you're a million miles away. I thought you were just as excited about being here as I am!"

"Holly, look over there! Do you see what I see?"

Holly peered over in the direction in which Chris was pointing, expecting to see some fabulous exhibit or an unusual space vehicle. Instead, all she saw was a group of tourists, shuffling along and looking awestruck, carrying guidebooks and cameras—just like hundreds of other people in the museum. Disappointed, she frowned.

"Chris, all I see is—"

But before she had a chance to finish, Chris interrupted her. "Holly, that's *her*! I *swear* that's her!"

"Who? What are you talking about? Who *is* that, Chris?"

"That's Natasha!"

"*Who?*" By now Holly was really confused.

"Natasha! Remember? The Russian ballerina I met at the airport yesterday?"

Suddenly it all made sense to Holly. She, too, grew excited.

"Oh, of course! How could I have forgotten? Which one is she?"

"The one with the dark brown hair, wearing the blue dress. At the back of the group. She's walking with her friend, Katya. See, the one with the blond hair."

"Well, then, why don't we show them how friendly Americans can be? Let's go over and say hello. I'd love it if you'd introduce us."

Warily, Chris looked around first, anxious to see if the man in the gray suit was near the group of Russian dancers. Sure enough, he was, although he was wearing a dark blue suit today. Alongside him walked a woman in a brown dress, wearing the same serious expression that he wore. Chris immediately surmised that she, too, was a chaperone for the group.

Even so, she thought, I shouldn't let them bother me. Holly is right. Natasha and I are *friends*, and there's no reason in the world why I shouldn't go over and say hello to her.

"Okay, Holly. Let's go!"

Wearing their biggest, friendliest smiles, Chris and Holly headed toward the group of Russian ballet dancers. They walked right over to Natasha and Katya.

Even before they had said hello, however, Natasha noticed Chris. She broke into a wide smile and said, "Christine Pratt! Hello! This is certainly—how you say—little world!"

"It *is* a small world," said Chris. "It's so nice to see you again, Natasha. This is my best friend, Holly."

"Hello, Holly. Christine, Holly, this is Katya. She is also ballet dancer."

"Hi, Katya. So, Natasha, how are you enjoying Washington so far?"

"Oh, very much! Is very beautiful city. And already we have seen so much! White House and Capitol, all this morning on bus tour. And now we are seeing wonderful museum of space travel."

"We've seen a lot, too," said Holly. "We took a tour of the whole city this morning, and we sat in on a session of Congress—"

"Natasha! Katya!"

All of a sudden, the four girls' congenial conversation was interrupted by a harsh voice. The woman Chris had noticed earlier, the one she had decided must be a second chaperone, came over and began scolding the two dancers in Russian. Natasha finally looked over at Chris and Holly and smiled apologetically.

"I am sorry, but we must go now. Mrs. Korsky reminds us that we have many more things to see today. And tonight we have dance rehearsal. We are very busy, so we must follow the schedule that has been planned for us."

Looking satisfied, the chaperone moved away. Chris was all set to say good-bye when Natasha reached into the bag she was carrying over her shoulder.

"I have something for you, Chris," she said softly. "I have little gift."

"A gift?" Chris blinked.

"Yes, because you are my first American friend. I planned to give it to you when our two tour groups met at the rehearsal tomorrow afternoon. But since I see you here by accident, I give gift to you now."

She took out a beautiful book on ballet, filled with large colorful photographs. "Perhaps looking at this book will help you enjoy the performance of *Coppelia* even more on Saturday night. Perhaps it will help make the evening more memorable."

Chris didn't know what to say. "I . . . you . . . Gee, Natasha, *thank* you!" She took the book and thumbed through it. "It's even in English!"

"I bought it for you this afternoon at one of the museum bookstores. Do you like it?"

"I love it! I can't wait to read it!"

"I am so pleased." Natasha placed her hand on Chris's arm and said, with great earnestness, "Just make sure you read it soon, Christine. By Saturday night, at the very latest."

Chris was a bit surprised by Natasha's vehemence, but she agreed. "Sure, Natasha. I'll take a look at it the very first chance I get. Tonight, even, after dinner, when we all get back to the hotel."

"Good. I am so pleased! That you like the book, I mean."

Natasha looked around, as if she were suddenly nervous. "There—that is done. Now we must go. We still have so much to do today."

With that, Natasha dashed off.

"Boy, that was sure nice of Natasha!" Chris was still marveling over her new friend's generosity as she tucked the book under her arm. "I mean, we hardly even know each other, yet here she is giving me presents."

Holly shrugged. "I guess she's taking this cultural exchange thing really seriously. She seems to think it's really important to make friends here in the United States."

"Well, I just wish there was something I could do for her in return," said Chris wistfully. "But I'll worry about that later. For now, let's get going! You and I have still got this whole museum to cover!"

As Chris and Holly returned to their sightseeing, full steam ahead, Natasha and her generous gift were forgotten. At least for now.

Four

"It was fabulous!*" cried Susan, plopping down on one* of the two single beds in the pleasant hotel room. "I've never seen such a magnificent museum in my entire life. They had everything: costumes, old political campaign buttons—"

"They even had an entire *street*, believe it or not," Beth interrupted excitedly. "It was made up to be an exact replica of the old-fashioned main streets that were in small towns back at the turn of the century. There was an apothecary shop, and an old-fashioned candy store, and a milliner's shop, full of the most outrageous hats you've ever seen. . . . It was like stepping back in time!"

It was Thursday evening, right after dinner, and the twins had gotten together with their friends in Chris and Holly's room to talk about all the things they'd seen and done that afternoon. They were all worn out, after having put in a full day of sightseeing around Washington. Even so, they managed to muster up the energy to show off the souvenirs they had acquired and exclaim over the wonders they had encountered while playing tourist.

"Wow, the American History Museum sounds great," said Holly. "I wish I had time to see it. But there's so much I want to see and do here. . . ."

"You should definitely check it out, Holly. You've got time. After all, it's only Thursday night. We still have all day Friday and Saturday left for sightseeing. That's two whole days."

"Well . . ."

"You should really go, Holly. You'd love it, I promise. Look, if I haven't managed to talk you into it yet, I'd like to show you a terrific book I got there." Beth was insistent. "It's filled with photographs of some of the exhibits they have at the museum. You're welcome to take a look at it."

"Okay. Then I'll have a better idea of whether or not to add it to my list."

"Great. It's in my room. Come on over, and I'll show it to you."

Once Chris and Susan were alone, Chris remembered the gift that Natasha had given her that afternoon.

"Hey, speaking of books, you'll never guess what happened today, Sooz!" She proceeded to tell her sister all about her chance meeting with the Russian ballerina and the beautiful picture book about ballet that her new friend had given her.

"Wow, that sure was nice of her," Susan commented. "After all, you two hardly even know each other."

"I know. It's a neat book, too. Wait until you see it."

Sitting side by side on the bed that Chris had been

using, the twins began leafing through the book, exclaiming over each photograph they came across. Many famous ballets were represented within its pages. The costumes were lovely, the sets were exquisite. And the dancers, of course, were magnificent.

"Hey, what's the name of the ballet we're seeing at the Kennedy Center this Saturday night?" Susan suddenly asked. "Did Natasha ever happen to mention which one they were doing?"

"As a matter of fact, she did. It's *Coppelia.*"

"Ooh, I love that one. It's about a doll who comes to life. Hey, let's look it up in this book. Wait—here it is."

As Susan turned to the page which, according to the book's index, featured photographs of the ballet that the Russian dancers would be performing in two nights, something caught Chris's eye. Stuck inside the book on that particular page was a slip of white paper, folded in half.

"Hey, what's this?" Puzzled, Chris took it out of the book.

"Oh, it's probably just the receipt, from when Natasha bought the book. Didn't you say she'd bought it for you just today?"

"Maybe I shouldn't look at it, then." Chris grinned. "After all, it *was* a gift."

Chris was about to toss the sheet of paper into the trash can, then reconsidered. She decided that she should at least glance at it, just to make sure it wasn't something important that Natasha had left in the book by mistake.

She unfolded the piece of paper, looked at it . . . and then immediately, she froze.

"Susan!" she cried after a few seconds. "*Look* at this!"

"What is it, Chris?"

Susan was actually concerned by the tone of her sister's voice, and the look on her face. She took the piece of paper away from her and glanced at it. And then she froze, too.

"I am planning to defect," the note read. "You must help me!"

After a long silence, during which the twins just kept staring at the note, Susan finally said, "What are we going to do, Chris?"

"I don't know, Sooz." Chris's voice was now a whisper. "Do you think it's a joke?"

"I don't think so. This hardly seems like the kind of thing somebody would joke about."

"Especially since Natasha and the others are always so closely watched by those two chaperones of theirs. That creepy Mr. Pirov and his sidekick, Mrs. Korsky." Chris gulped. "She sure was taking a big risk by getting this note to us."

Susan and Chris looked at each other.

"Chris, are you thinking what I'm thinking?"

"I am if what you're thinking is that this isn't a hoax, but that Natasha is serious. *Very* serious."

Susan nodded. "And I'll tell you something else I'm thinking. You and I may have played our share of pranks in the past, and sometimes we've even managed to help some people out. But I think you've got to agree with me when I say that this time, we're dealing with something that's over our heads."

"*Way* over our heads." Chris's heart was pounding as she looked at the note one more time. "As a matter of fact, Sooz, I think the best thing for us to do is just forget all about this. Pretend it never even happened. And no matter what, never, *ever* mention it to Natasha."

And to illustrate how serious she was about what she had just said, Chris folded the note in half once again and ripped it up into a dozen tiny pieces. And then, with great ceremony, she walked over to the bathroom and flushed it down the toilet.

When she came back into the bedroom, the expression on her face was one of dead seriousness.

"Let's make a pact, Sooz. A pact that says we'll never mention this to anybody, okay? Not to Holly, not to Beth . . ."

"Not even to each other. Like you said before, we'll never talk about it again, period." Susan shuddered. "After all, we wouldn't want anything to happen to Natasha!"

Just then, Holly and Beth burst into the room.

"I'm definitely going to the Museum of American History," Holly cried. "The book that Beth bought there convinced me that I simply shouldn't miss it. It sounds fantastic. First thing tomorrow, the minute they open up the doors. Want to come along, Chris?"

Now that Beth and Holly were back, Chris and Susan could no longer talk about Natasha's haunting note. Instead, for the rest of the evening, the girls chattered away, all about their plans for the next few days' sightseeing.

Even so, neither Chris nor Susan could forget it.

That night, after they'd gone to bed, both of the twins lay awake for a long time, Chris in the hotel room she was sharing with Holly, Susan in the room she and Beth were in. They were both unable to sleep, too wrapped up in thinking about Natasha and her plight to relax.

Susan was troubled, but relieved that she and her sister had agreed that this was one situation that was way out of their league. The pact the two of them made was definitely a good idea, she was sure. Sure, she could imagine how Natasha was feeling, but helping a Russian ballerina defect was just a bit too much, even for this prank-playing team!

Chris, on the other hand, was also thinking about the pact she and Susan had made—a pact that had been her idea in the first place. But now that she had a chance to think about it, her reaction was a little bit different from her twin sister's.

Gee, I feel bad for Natasha, she was thinking. She must really want to leave Russia, to come live here in America, if she's willing to take a risk like trying to defect! Not to mention how hard it must be to leave behind everything that's familiar to her, forever and ever. . . .

Finally, Chris did manage to fall asleep. But not before she began to wonder if maybe—*maybe*—there might be some way, however small, that she and Susan could put their heads together and help.

Five

Georgetown, the section of Washington, D.C., that was surrounded by the buildings of Georgetown University, was a haven for shoppers. True, its quaint brownstones, red brick sidewalks, and tree-lined streets made the area the perfect place for a leisurely stroll on a pleasant spring morning. But it was the endless supply of shops—clothing boutiques, bookstores, cafés, French and Italian restaurants, and just about everything else imaginable—that lured Susan and Beth to this picturesque neighborhood the very first thing on Friday morning.

"I'm glad we decided to start out early," commented Beth as the two girls rode up the escalator, out of the sleek, modern underground rapid-transit-system station. "Stopping for breakfast in Georgetown, instead of having eaten back at the hotel, will be much more interesting. And then we can get down to some serious shopping right away!"

"Maybe we can even find an outdoor café," Susan

said hopefully. "Wouldn't it be fun to sit outside and watch all the people go by while we have breakfast?"

It wasn't long before the girls happened upon the perfect place. They had a relaxed breakfast at a charming outdoor café, meanwhile watching all the people who passed by: university students, casual strollers, tourists, businesspeople hurrying off to work. By the time they had finished, they couldn't wait to start exploring this vibrant district of the city, and, as Beth had put it, do some "serious shopping."

"Ooh, look at this shop!" Susan exclaimed before the two of them had wandered very far beyond the café. "It has such cute clothes in the window. I love those blouses over there. Let's go in."

Over the next hour, Beth and Susan went inside almost two dozen stores. Beth was looking for a birthday present for her mother, and in one of the boutiques, she found the perfect item: a beautiful hand-painted silk scarf. Susan, on the other hand, didn't have anything in particular she wanted to buy. She was simply keeping her eyes open for something unusual, something distinctive; something useful that would be a "souvenir," reminding her of her trip every time she used it.

She was on the verge of giving up, however, when she and Beth came across still one more clothing store, this one featuring bright, trendy fashions for young people. The windows were filled with pretty spring clothes, and it was almost impossible not to venture inside to get a better look at the shop's merchandise.

"We'll just take a peek," Susan insisted. "We've been scouring the stores all morning, and I'm just about ready to move on. Besides, don't forget that I'm meeting

Chris for lunch at the National Gallery of Art at one o'clock. But I think we can take a quick look around."

"Relax. We've still got plenty of time," Beth assured her after glancing at her watch. "Hey, this is a great store. Maybe you'll find whatever it is you've been looking for in here."

Sure enough, it wasn't long before Susan came across a rack of cotton T-shirt dresses in pretty colors. The dresses were soft, comfortable, practical; just the thing to wear to school, or even to a place that called for a more dressed-up outfit.

"Look at these," Susan called to Beth, who was browsing through a rack of sundresses, in anticipation of the summer ahead. "Aren't they cute?"

"Oh, yes!" Beth came over immediately. "They come in such nice colors! I like the blue, and this purple. . . . But this pink one is my favorite."

"They're the color of pink lemonade!" Susan commented with a chuckle. She couldn't help thinking of the conversation between Natasha and Chris that her twin had related to her on Wednesday evening, when they'd first arrived at Washington's airport. "It's the perfect shade for spring. Come on, let's try them on. What size do you need?"

Both Beth and Susan fell in love with the dresses as soon as they slipped them on in the store's dressing room and stepped in front of a mirror. They were simple, cut just like short-sleeved T-shirts; only they looked as if they had kept on growing at the hem.

"I'm going to get one," Beth declared, turning around in front of the mirror so she could check out the back. "How about you?"

"I'm going to get *two*."

"*Two?*"

"That's right," said Susan. "One for me, and one for Chris. We don't usually have the same taste in clothes, but I have a feeling she's going to be crazy about this dress. And I know she loves pink."

"I can already picture how she'll look in it, too," Beth joked. "Funny, but I'm having no trouble imagining Chris in that dress."

Susan laughed. "Just one of the bonuses of shopping for an identical twin sister. But don't forget that while *I'll* probably wear this dress with a simple string of white beads, *Chris* will no doubt wear hers with a purple belt, yellow shoes, and turquoise blue earrings!"

After the girls had left the dressing room, they were so enthusiastic about the dresses they had found that they decided to take one more quick look around the store, just in case there was something else on the racks that they had missed. Beth headed toward the back, a section filled with spring jackets and raincoats. Susan, meanwhile, went up to the front, for a more thorough look at the sportswear that was on display.

It was while she was going through a rack of sweatshirts that she suddenly began to get the funny feeling that she was being watched. At first, she just ignored it, figuring that either she was just imagining it or else that a salesperson, or perhaps another shopper, was standing behind her. But the creepy feeling didn't go away.

Finally, she whirled around. And even though she had been half expecting to find herself face to face with someone, she jumped.

The person who had been watching her was a man in a

dark suit, wearing a very serious expression and looking straight at Susan.

"So, Christine Pratt, we meet again," the man said. He had a very thick accent, one that Susan knew right away was Russian.

Her first impulse was to correct him, to tell him that she wasn't Christine at all. But part of her was still too startled to say anything. And another part of her had a feeling that the best thing to do was just go along with it—at least, for now.

"H-hello," she said quietly.

"I am glad that I happened to run into you like this today," the man said.

Susan's mouth dropped open. She sincerely doubted that a meeting between Christine Pratt, the brand-new American friend of the Russian ballerina Natasha, and the ballet troupe's stern chaperone was merely a coincidence! Especially since that meeting was taking place in a young women's clothing boutique! But she said nothing.

"There is something I would like to tell you, now that you and I are having this unexpected opportunity to chat together."

"Yes?" Susan said sweetly. "What would you like to tell me?"

Very calmly, the man said, "If you know what is best for everybody, Christine, you will keep away from Natasha."

Susan just stared at him and kept listening.

"I have been noticing that you two keep running into each other by accident." With a funny smile, he added, "Very much like the way I just 'happened' to run into you today."

Susan gulped.

"This mixing together in such a manner is not something that we approve of."

Suddenly Susan stopped being frightened of this man. Instead she felt a surge of anger rise up from deep inside her.

"Wait a minute. One of the reasons the kids from my school *came* to Washington was to 'mix' with the members of the ballet troupe! And now you're telling me to keep away, that you don't approve—"

The man held up his hand, as if to stop her from going on.

"Ah, you misunderstand me, Christine." His voice was now softer, and more kind, but the tone underlying what he was saying had not changed at all. "Of course we are here so Russian young people are able to meet American young people. We are always anxious to encourage good international relations. However, Miss Pratt, you know as well as I do that this cultural exchange program that has been planned for us all is not what I am referring to."

"Oh, really? Then what exactly *are* you referring to, may I ask?"

Even as she feigned innocence, Susan was thinking about the note she and Chris had found in Natasha's book, just the night before. She looked around, hoping that Beth might be wandering over in her direction and would soon interrupt this conversation, which was making her more and more uncomfortable with each passing minute. But unfortunately her friend was nowhere nearby.

"You know, Miss Pratt," the man went on, leaning

forward slightly and lowering his voice, "we already know all about you."

" 'We?' " Susan blinked.

But the man didn't bother to explain. He simply stared at her coldly.

"You are Christine Elizabeth Pratt, and you live with your parents in Whittington," he said smugly. "You attend Whittington High School, where you are a senior."

Susan thought about what he had just said, and then looked him in the eye. "Hey, wait a minute. Sure you know all that about me, but you haven't told me a single fact that wouldn't be obvious to just about anyone. After all, your dancers *are* here as part of that cultural exchange program with the Whittington High School students, and I wouldn't be surprised if there was a list my school had given you that had every one of those facts on it."

"Ah, you are a very clever girl. But then again, we have suspected that for quite some time already. You want more proof, do you? You need further indication that we have easy access to much information about you, Christine Pratt? All right, then.

"You have a sister named Susan. You are cheerleader at your school, and also you are on your school's swimming team. You have many friends, and great interest in the rock music. Last summer, you worked as counselor at camp called Camp Pinewood. . . ."

Susan's mouth dropped open. So this man wasn't bluffing, after all! He *did* have access to all kinds of information about her. Not only that; he had gone ahead and researched her background! It was a frightening thought.

But then, all of a sudden, she realized that this man may have been pretending to know everything there was to know about her . . . yet he had left out one very important fact.

He hadn't realized that Christine and Susan were identical twins.

And beyond that, he had no idea that this wasn't even Christine Pratt that he was talking to!

Susan was tempted to burst out laughing. But she didn't. She liked the idea of having "secrets" from this man. Especially since he was so certain he knew everything there was to know about her.

So, instead, she put on her most serious expression and said, "Goodness. I can see that you *do* know quite a bit about me."

The Russian man looked satisfied. He folded his arms across his chest and nodded.

"Da. I am only telling you this so you will know that I am serious, that, as you say here in United States, 'I mean business' when I say that it will be best for everyone if from now on you keep away from Natasha."

Susan pretended to think about that for a moment.

"I understand what you're saying perfectly, and I'm willing to keep away from her, just to prove to you that you're imagining things. But won't it look kind of funny if during our cultural exchange events—you know, the dance rehearsal and the party before Saturday night's performance—I make a point of avoiding Natasha? Especially since I've already told everyone that we're friends. I mean, what will everybody think?"

The man's eyes narrowed into two tiny slits. "Of course this is problem. And you are very wise to think of this. But there is simple solution. When you see

Natasha, you are to be nice to her. But do not forget for an instant that we will be watching you closely. *Very* closely."

He bent forward then, so that his face was very close to Susan's. "But most important, Christine, it will be best if you do not go out of your way to see Natasha at any other time. I think you understand what I am saying."

"Oh, yes," Susan said evenly. "I understand completely."

Just then, she spotted Beth, making her way toward her across the store. At first Susan was relieved; after all, having Beth come over and start talking to her would put an end to this most unpleasant conversation. But then she realized that if Beth called her by name, the "chaperone" would realize that she had been tricking him. And she had a funny feeling that he wouldn't like that one bit.

"Gee, here comes my friend," she said hastily, moving away from the man and pretending to be looking through a rack of pastel-colored jeans. "I guess I'd better be moving along. But I'm sure I'll be seeing you again soon. . . ."

By the time Susan turned around, the man was gone.

"Hey, who was that you were talking to?" Beth asked as she caught up with Susan. She wrinkled up her nose and added, "He looked kind of strange."

Susan's first instinct was to make up a story about how he was just some stranger, asking directions or just chatting. But then she remembered that between the upcoming dance rehearsal and the party Saturday night, there was a good chance that Beth would be meeting the Russian dancers' chaperone. After all, it was becoming increasing clear that these "chaperones" were very much committed to keeping track of everything the young Russians did—and everyone they came into contact with.

"Oh, apparently he's one of the chaperones who came along on the trip with those Russian ballet dancers we're supposed to be meeting," Susan said, trying to sound very casual about the whole incident. "He thought I was Chris." Immediately she went on to say, "Hey, look at these lavender jeans. What a great color!"

But Beth wasn't as willing to let the incident pass as she had hoped.

"What do you mean, he thought you were Chris?" she said. "You don't look anything at all like Chris today! Well, hardly, anyway. I mean, it's not as if he spotted you across the room and recognized you immediately."

Susan shrugged. "Maybe you just think that because you know us both so well."

"Maybe." Beth thought for a minute. "Hey, I know!" she said after a moment, her face lighting up. "I'll bet he *followed* you here from the hotel! Wow, wouldn't that be something?"

Susan pretended to be scornful of this theory. "Oh, come on, Beth. What on earth *for*?" This time she was insistent about changing the subject. "Hey, we'd better get going. If I'm late for my lunch date with Chris, she'll never forgive me."

The two girls headed toward the cash register, anxious to pay for the three dresses and be on their way. Beth, it seemed, forgot all about the "coincidence," the chance meeting between the Russian and the Christine Pratt look-alike, as she started counting out her money, suddenly concerned about whether she would have enough.

Susan, on the other hand, had done anything *but* forget about it. As a matter of fact, as she left the store and headed back toward the Mall, where she was meeting her sister for lunch, she could scarcely wait to tell Chris all about it.

Six

"*Chris, never in a million* years *are you going to guess* what just happened!"

Christine Pratt surveyed her sister, noticed the shopping bag she was carrying, and said, "Don't tell me. You just discovered the biggest bargain of the century."

Susan couldn't help chuckling as she dropped into a chair opposite her twin. It was just past one o'clock, and Susan had just arrived at the new wing of the National Gallery of Art, where she and her sister had planned to meet for lunch.

The girls were sitting at a small round table in the café located on the balcony, overlooking the center of the building. The modern building was awe-inspiring, with its clean, simple lines and odd geometric shape. As if that weren't enough, all around them were impressive works of art. Sitting at the café afforded them a magnificent view of a huge metal Calder sculpture, a mobile made of colorful shapes that turned in a slow, hypnotic fashion, hovering alongside the balcony.

But art was the last thing on the girls' minds at the moment. Chris was interested only in food, while Susan was almost ready to burst with her news of what had happened to her earlier that day in Georgetown.

And so she was a bit taken back when, the moment she sat down and tucked her shopping bag under her chair, Chris thrust a menu at her.

"Here. You look like you need food. You've got that crazed look that shoppers always get whenever they manage to find something they're crazy about—for half the regular price."

Susan, however, ignored the menu. "Chris, listen to me! This is important!"

"Sure it is," Chris interrupted her. "Just tell me one thing: What's in the shopping bag?"

"Dresses," Susan replied impatiently. "Two pink T-shirt dresses."

"Two?"

"Yes, Chris. One for me and one for you."

"For *me*! Oh, Sooz, you shouldn't have! Can I see it? Please?"

"Chris, *forget* the dresses, for now, anyway. Listen to me. This morning—just about an hour ago, in fact—while Beth and I were shopping in a little store in Georgetown, all of a sudden this man came up and started talking to me. . . ."

"Don't tell me," Chris joked. "He tried to talk you into getting some blue shoes to go with the dress."

By this point, Susan was growing completely exasperated with her twin.

"He said he was a friend of Natasha's."

Chris immediately grew serious, and was willing to listen to her sister in earnest for the first time since Susan had sat down at the table.

"A friend . . . of Natasha's?" Chris blinked.

"Well, not a friend, exactly. . . . But are you finally ready to listen to me?"

"I sure am! I'm all ears! What happened? What did he say?"

"Oh, gee," Susan said loftily, now reaching for the menu she'd pushed aside only moments earlier. "I'm so darned *thirsty* all of a sudden! Let's see; what have they got here to drink?"

"Sooz . . ."

"Iced tea, coffee . . . oh, look! They have lemonade. I wonder if it's *pink* lemonade."

"Susan Pratt! You'd better tell me this *instant* what the man said to you!"

Susan could keep up her teasing no longer. She leaned forward and, in a voice soft enough that no one at the other tables nearby could hear, said, "Oh, Chris, he *threatened* me!"

"What are you talking about?" Chris, too, was talking softly. Her voice was nothing more than a hoarse whisper. "Do you mean he *knows* about Natasha's note?"

"I don't think so." Susan frowned as she thought for a few seconds. "And I have a feeling that he would have said something if he *did* know."

Just then, a waitress came by to take their order. By now the twins were hardly interested in food at all. They glanced at their menus, quickly chose salads for their lunches, and immediately went back to their conversation—after looking around and checking, one more time, to make sure that no one was listening to them.

"So what did he *say*?" Chris demanded. Then, almost to herself, she said, "I bet he was that chaperone of theirs, the one I heard scolding that dancer, Ivan, when he started to wander away at the airport. That mean-looking Mr. Pirov. And then I saw him again at the Air and Space Museum. . . . What did he look like, anyway, Sooz?"

Susan described the man who had sought her out in the clothing store, and Chris agreed that he was, indeed, one of the Russian ballet troupe's two chaperones. Then Susan went on to relate exactly what had happened: how he had approached her; how he had assumed she was Chris, and how she had played along with his assumption; how in the course of proving how much he already knew about her, he had never mentioned the fact that Christine Pratt had an identical twin sister.

"Wow!" Chris breathed, once her twin was finished. The waitress came by with their salads then, so she had a minute to think about everything she had just been told. "That really is amazing, Sooz! He obviously thinks that the two chance meetings between Natasha and me were planned. I mean, it sounds as if he actually believes that there's something funny going on here!"

Susan's response was a grin. "Well, he's right, in a way, isn't he? After all, there *is* something going on. At least, *now* there is!"

Chris just looked puzzled.

"The note, remember?"

"Oh, yes. The note." Chris was lost in thought for a few seconds. "Do you know what, Sooz? I have a feeling that that man who's been keeping such a close watch on Natasha—*and* me—is more than just a chaperone."

Susan's brown eyes opened wide. "More? What do you mean, Chris?"

Chris looked around the restaurant one more time. At the table on the twins' immediate right was a couple in their thirties, who looked more interested in holding hands under the table than in eavesdropping on other people's conversations. On the right was a family, a mother, father, and two little boys under the age of ten, busily studying a map of the city, trying to decide whether or not to head for the zoo next. She decided it was safe enough to speak freely. Even so, she leaned forward, narrowed her eyes, and spoke very, very softly.

"I think he may work for the government," she said seriously. "He could well be a member of the KGB. You know, the Russian secret police."

Susan nearly fell off her chair. "Chris! Are you serious?"

Chris, still wearing that same earnest expression, just nodded. "Of course, I don't know for *sure* . . . and we'll probably never know. But one thing's for certain. The troupe's 'chaperone' is taking more than just a passing interest in what Natasha Samchenko does."

Susan had to agree. "He does seem to be very involved in checking up on her, doesn't he?"

The two girls lapsed into silence. For the first time since their waitress had delivered their lunches to their table, they actually began eating. Thoughtfully they picked at their food, barely tasting the carefully prepared dish.

And then, at almost exactly the same time, Susan and Chris both spoke.

"Do you know what . . ." said Chris.

"I've been thinking . . ." Susan began.

They started to laugh, then quickly grew serious.

"I wonder if you and I were about to say the same thing," Chris mused, putting down her fork.

Susan smiled. "It wouldn't be the first time, Chris. You and I sometimes seem to have a 'sixth sense' about what the other is thinking."

"Especially when we've both been thinking about the same problem." Chris took a deep breath. "Well, I'll go first. I know that you and I agreed that this whole thing with Natasha was something way over our heads—"

"Something too dangerous for us to get involved in," Susan interjected helpfully. "Yes, that's what you and I had decided, as of last night."

"It's funny, though: After what just happened, with that 'chaperone' or whatever he is warning us, saying that I'd better keep away from Natasha, I'm beginning to wonder if what we decided is the right thing, after all."

Susan nodded. "I know what you mean. It seems that you and I are getting more and more involved in this every minute, anyway. Besides," she added with an impish grin, "you know as well as I do that once someone insists that the Pratt twins keep out of something, it's impossible for us to resist doing just that!"

The girls burst out laughing, since they knew she was right. It was true that Chris and Susan weren't at all the type to turn their backs on a challenge.

Susan looked at her sister and said, "Okay, now what? So we've decided to help Natasha, no matter what happens, no matter who threatens us. But where do we go from here?"

Chris shook her head. "I wish I knew, Sooz. We'll just

have to put our heads together and try to come up with something. But in the meantime, we've got to let Natasha know that we found her note in that book she gave me, and that we have every intention of doing our darndest to help her!"

"Hmmm." Susan was pensive as she toyed with her salad. "That probably won't be easy. Especially since that snoop is no doubt going to be keeping his eye on you. . . ."

"Sooz, that's it!" Chris grabbed her sister's arm so abruptly that a forkful of lettuce and a cherry tomato went flying across the table, onto the floor.

Susan looked at her twin in bewilderment. "*What's* it, Chris?"

"What you just said. That Natasha's chaperone is going to be keeping his eye on *me*."

"Sorry, Chris. I still don't get it."

Chris just smiled. "Just leave it to me. I'll fill you in on the details later. Because, let's face it, if we're really going to go through with this, we'd better start being a lot more careful about what we say—and where we say it."

Susan started to protest, then realized that her sister could well be right. If they were going to help the ballerina defect from the Soviet Union while she was in Washington, being as cautious as possible was crucial for *everyone's* sake.

"Besides," Chris went on, her voice now teasing, "you still haven't told me very much about the new dress you bought me!"

"Oh, it's really cute. I'm sure you'll love it. As a matter of fact, Beth got one, too."

"You two shoppers bought *three* of the same dress?" Chris squealed.

Susan couldn't help laughing. "That's right. We practically bought out the entire store! Here, I'll show you."

She opened up the shopping bag and took out one of the pink dresses. Chris agreed right away that it was definitely her style.

"And I love the color," she exclaimed. "That shade of pink is gorgeous!"

"What does it remind you of?" Susan asked with a twinkle in her eye.

Chris thought for only a few seconds. "Why, pink lemonade, of course!" She burst out laughing.

"Hey, Chris, what's so funny?" a masculine voice suddenly broke in.

"Yeah, Chris. How about you and Susan sharing the joke with us?"

Surprised, Susan and Chris turned around. Standing behind them, wearing huge grins, were Gary Graham and Tim Patterson.

"Tim! Gary! What are *you* doing here?" Chris exclaimed.

"No doubt exactly the same thing *you're* doing," Gary returned.

Susan and Chris looked at each other in surprise, then realized what Gary meant and started to chuckle.

"Hey, what's up?" Gary asked, looking puzzled. "*Now* what's so funny?"

"Oh, nothing," Susan replied. "I guess what you meant is that you're here to see the museum, just as we are."

"Well, sure," said Tim. "You girls haven't already made the grand tour of this place, have you?"

"No. Sooz and I just got here a little while ago. We thought we'd stuff our faces first, to make sure we have plenty of energy. We still hope to spend a couple of hours here, before going on to the dance rehearsal later on this afternoon."

"Oh, yeah. That's today, isn't it?" said Tim. "I almost forgot."

"I guess that should be pretty interesting," Gary observed. "I understand that ballet dancers are amazing athletes. They may manage to make all that stuff they do look easy, but it requires lots of strength and stamina—not to mention practice!"

"Well, then, why don't we start that 'grand tour' of this museum right away?" suggested Susan. "I know I've eaten just about all the lettuce I can handle right now. That is, whatever lettuce managed to stay on the table. I'm ready for some art!"

"Me, too," her twin agreed with a chuckle. "After all, those Russian dancers may have a lot of strength and stamina, but when it comes to being a tourist, nobody beats the Pratt twins! Let's pay the check and go!"

Arm in arm, Tim and Susan led the way, with Gary and Chris close behind them. But even as they chatted gaily with the boys, the twins' thoughts were heavy. Before, thinking about Natasha's plan to defect had just been something to make them feel sympathy for the girl's situation. Now that they had decided to become involved in it themselves, however, the real seriousness of it—not to mention the danger—was beginning to hit them for the very first time.

Seven

"So, Chris, are you having a good time here in Washington?" asked Holly, knowing full well what her best friend's answer was going to be.

The two girls had just joined the rest of the Whittington High School students who were piling onto the specially chartered bus. They were all headed for what promised to be one of the highlights of their trip to Washington, D.C. This afternoon, they were going to a dance studio, where they would have the opportunity to watch the Russian visitors rehearse for their gala performance.

And Chris was at least as excited as everyone else. So far, their trip had been as much fun as she had hoped . . . and even more exciting than she had ever dreamed.

"I'm having a great time!" Chris assured her friend heartily. "Why, I've already seen so much. Museums and monuments and of course the White House . . ."

"What about Skip Desmond?" Holly teased. "Have you been seeing much of him?"

"Hah!" Chris didn't know whether to laugh or to be indignant. "Fortunately, he's left me alone during this entire trip. I'm so relieved that he hasn't been bothering me. I must admit, I've been just a little bit worried about him, ever since that day he pushed me and all my books ended up on the floor."

"Maybe he's been too busy learning all about our nation's government to have any time left over for romance."

"Or maybe he's finally realized that this 'crush' you claim he has on me is simply a waste of time. At any rate," Chris went on, waving her hand in the air as if to dismiss the unpleasant subject of Skip Desmond, "I've been having the time of my life, running around Washington, sightseeing, and just having fun."

"Yes," Holly went on, a bit more seriously, "but has all this sightseeing helped lift you out of that blue mood you were in a few weeks ago? You haven't said a word about it, not since that day you had that run-in with Skip."

It was true; Chris had been so busy enjoying herself, and thinking about Natasha, too, of course—that she had forgotten all about her concerns about her future. Susan, of course, was already waiting anxiously for the decisions from the admissions committees of the art schools to which she'd applied, telephoning her mother every chance she got to ask if anything had arrived in the mail yet. Chris, too, expected to hear from the colleges she'd applied to any day now. But ever since her arrival in Washington, all that had taken a back seat to everything that was happening to her here and now.

"As a matter of fact, Holly," Chris admitted with a chuckle, "I've been too busy having fun to give much thought to my plans for after graduation. Although I must admit that one thing *has* occurred to me. . . ."

But before she could finish, Ms. Parker announced that the Potomac River would best be seen from the left side of the bus. Chris and Holly immediately scrambled toward the opposite side of the bus, along with just about everyone else. For now at least, the subject of Chris's future was forgotten.

It was only a short ride to the dance studio, and it passed quickly as Chris and the others kept their noses pressed to the bus windows, anxious to see everything as they traveled through downtown Washington. They were almost disappointed when the bus finally stopped in front of a huge building, the size of a small warehouse, until they remembered what they had come here for.

"Boy, I can't wait to watch this dance rehearsal!" Holly exclaimed as she rushed to climb off the bus.

"Me, either," Chris agreed. "I love watching dancers. Every move they make is so graceful."

"And I love the way they dress when they're practicing, too." Susan, who had been sitting in back with Beth, joined her twin as soon as she got off the bus. As usual, the two of them were dressed so differently that it wasn't at all apparent that they were identical twins. "They always look so serious about their art, wrapped up in those ragged leg warmers and all, with their hair pulled back into those tight buns." She sighed wistfully. "Gee, maybe I should try making some sketches of them. I wish I'd thought of bringing along a sketch pad. . . .

Her twin cast her a warning look. This was no time for

that, they both knew. Not today, when the two of them had a much more important mission to carry out. And Susan hardly needed to be reminded of that.

It was that mission, in fact, that was first and foremost in her mind as the girls filed into the dance studio. And so she tensed up as soon as she and her twin entered the huge empty dance studio, past the receptionist, and saw Mr. Pirov, the "chaperone" who the girls were convinced was really a government agent, a member of the KGB, standing there, his arms folded firmly across his chest, his expression stern. Susan immediately dashed down a side corridor, grabbing her sister's arm as she did.

"Sooz! What are you trying to do, stretch out the yarn?" With a frown, Chris smoothed the sleeve of her purple-and-red-striped sweater. "Grandma knitted this sweater for me! It's one of my favorites!"

"Christine Pratt, this is no time to be discussing fashion!" Susan whispered hoarsely. She sounded as if she were on the edge of panic. "Did you see what I saw?"

"Of course I did, Sooz." Chris sounded as if she had everything under control. "The situation here is exactly what I expected it to be."

"Oh, really? You mean you're not surprised that Mr. Pirov is standing right here in the middle of everything, watching every move we make, listening to every word we say, practically?"

"Of course I'm not surprised." Chris did indeed sound perfectly calm. "After all, by this point I've already learned that everywhere that Natasha and the other Russian dancers are, Mr. Pirov and his pal Mrs. Korsky are bound to be pretty close behind."

"You've got a point there. . . . But what are we going to *do*, Chris?"

"What we *always* do in these sticky situations, Sooz."

"Oh, really? And what, may I ask, is that?"

Chris sounded matter-of-fact. "We'll outsmart them, of course. Don't forget," she added with a confident smile, "there are *two* of us. That means that two great minds are working on the problem."

Susan thought for a moment, and her frown turned to a smile. "I get it. And there are two identical faces to carry out whatever scheme we come up with!" she finished with a chuckle. "Okay, Chris. I'll go along with whatever you say. Just tell me: What's the plan?"

"Okay. It's pretty straightforward. You create a scene—you know, make a lot of noise, do something you're not supposed to be doing, anything—to divert everyone's attention. Meanwhile—"

"But Chris!" Susan protested. "You know I hate to be the center of attention!"

Her sister cast her a woeful look. "Well, if it's any consolation, you're going to be pretending that you're *me*. Just create the kind of commotion that Christine Pratt wouldn't think *twice* about creating."

Susan thought for a few seconds, then nodded her head. "I've got it. If I start feeling shy, I'll just remind myself that I'm not me, I'm you."

"Believe it or not, that makes perfect sense. Besides," Chris went on, "if you start feeling self-conscious, you can always remind yourself that this is all for a good cause. A *very* good cause."

By that point, Susan felt as if she were ready for

anything. "Okay, Chris. I've got the first part of the plan down. Then what?"

"Okay, Sooz. Now, while you're creating that commotion, and both the chaperones are concentrating on *you*, I'll sneak over to Natasha and tell her that I—I mean, we—have decided to help her out."

Susan nodded. "Got it. It's the best kind of plan, Chris. It's a *simple* plan."

"I know. Now," Chris mused with a sigh, "if only we could come up with a plan that would actually help Natasha defect!"

The girls' opportunity to let Natasha know that they planned to do their very best to help her with her secret—and terribly dangerous—plan came soon enough. A few seconds after Chris and Susan moved apart, not wanting to draw attention to the fact that they were identical twins, the Russian dancers began streaming into the studio, coming in through a wide door at the back.

At first, the twins were so enthralled by watching them that they forgot all about their mission. After all, there was so much to take in.

The girls were dressed in leotards, colorful leg warmers, and tights, theatrical getups that immediately created an air of excitement. The boys, meanwhile, wore tights and white T-shirts. All of them looked strong and agile and very graceful.

As soon as they came in, they headed directly for the wooden barre lining three walls of the dance studio and began stretching. It was amazing to see how easily they contorted their lean muscular torsos and limbs, bending in half and lifting their legs high onto the barre. And every move they made was beautiful, so fluid and controlled that they made the whole thing look simple.

Throughout it all, the dancers kept one eye on the mirror, anxious to check their form as they warmed up.

"Boy, they really are athletes, aren't they!" breathed Tim. There was real admiration in his voice.

"I'll say!" Gary agreed. "Gee, just look at the leg muscles on that guy over there! He makes the guys on the Whittington High School football team look like wimps!"

When Natasha strode into the dance studio a minute or two later, Chris and Susan exchanged meaningful glances. The graceful young dancer, her head held high and her movement fluid, seemed not to notice the crowd of Whittington High School students sitting on the floor in one corner of the large rehearsal hall. But the twins suspected that she did. After all, when she took her place at the barre, she chose a spot that was right in front of Chris. Once she was involved in her warm-up, she caught her friend's eye, but only for a fleeting moment. Even so, Chris was certain she knew exactly what Natasha was trying to say to her.

Susan noticed, too. Suddenly, without even thinking about feeling self-conscious or shy, she sprang up, dashed over to the barre, and took a place next to Katya, Natasha's friend.

And then, in her best and her *loudest* imitation of Chris Pratt at her most boisterous, she cried, "Hey, look at me! I can do this, too!"

With that, she threw her leg up on the barre in the same manner as Katya, and began imitating the stretching exercises that the professional dancers were doing with such grace and beauty.

Chris was so stunned by her sister's outrageous behavior that it took her a few seconds to remember that this was all part of the little plan the two of them had just worked out. But once she did, she didn't waste another moment.

As soon as Susan—or Chris, as far as Mr. Pirov and everyone else were concerned—headed toward the Russian dancers, the two chaperones jumped into action. They both hurried over to the bold American girl who had just taken it upon herself to join the Russian ballet troupe.

"What do you think you are doing?" shouted Mr. Pirov.

"Get away from there! Go sit down with the others!" insisted Mrs. Korsky, the heavy-set woman at his side.

Susan, however, kept on, imitating the dancers with exaggerated movements.

Chris glanced at her twin one more time, just to make sure that the attention of the two chaperones—as well as everyone else in the room, both the American students and the Russian dancers—was upon Susan. And, indeed, everyone was watching her, fascinated even as they were horrified by what she was doing.

Everyone, that is, except for Natasha. She was looking at Chris, her eyes pleading. Chris stood up and took two steps, which brought her right alongside the pretty, dark-haired dancer.

"Please?" said Natasha, her big brown eyes open wide. Her voice was barely a whisper.

"We got your note," Chris said softly. "And we'll help."

At this point, Natasha didn't seem at all surprised by Chris's use of the word *we*. She looked at Susan, then back at Chris. And she broke into a huge grin.

"You are twins!" Natasha sounded gleeful.

Chris nodded. "Yes. My sister's name is Susan. And we're *both* going to help you."

The Russian girl grew serious once again. "How? What is your plan?"

"I don't know yet. But don't worry; we'll think of something. We still have two days. . . ."

Before she could go on, however, Chris noticed that Susan was no longer at the barre carrying on and creating the distraction she needed in order to talk to Natasha. She had been led away by Ms. Parker, then firmly told to sit down with the other Whittington High students.

Quickly Chris sat down again. As soon as she did, she glanced over at Susan, who by now was also sitting with the group. Her cheeks were a bright shade of pink, but Chris couldn't tell if that was from embarrassment or from triumph. Quickly she looked over at Mr. Pirov and Mrs. Korsky. They were both scowling.

But Chris couldn't have been happier. As a matter of fact, she felt like bursting into song, or at least jumping up and down. After all, she and her twin had just outsmarted the entire Russian security system!

Now, she thought ruefully, turning her attention back to the dance rehearsal and wondering if she would ever be able to concentrate, if only Sooz and I can keep on doing just that!

Eight

"Well, now, that went pretty smoothly!" Susan exclaimed triumphantly.

It was Friday night, a few hours after the dancers' rehearsal and the twins' success with telling Natasha that they were, indeed, willing to help her out. They were back at the hotel, tired after the long day, but more than a little jubilant about the afternoon's accomplishment. This was the first chance they'd had to talk out of earshot of their fellow Whittington High students, Russian dancers, and, especially, the "chaperones."

"So tell me, Chris," Susan went on anxiously. "Was I okay? Did I do a good enough job?"

"Are you kidding? You sure did!" Chris assured her. "Why, you were fantastic! You acted so outrageously that everyone was watching you, including Mr. Pirov and Mrs. Korsky. I had enough time to tell Natasha that we'd decided to help her, and I'm positive that not one person noticed a thing."

She hesitated for a moment, then said, "Hey, Sooz?"

"Yes?"

"You don't *really* think I'd ever do anything as outlandish as that, do you? I mean, I know you were pretending you were me and all, and thinking about that *was* supposed to make you brave enough to do something really crazy, but . . ."

"Of course not! You may be a trifle more adventurous than most girls your age, Chris, but you're definitely too well mannered and too levelheaded ever to try a stunt like that."

Chris couldn't help feeling relieved. "I'm glad to hear that, Sooz. I was really beginning to wonder there for a minute. Now," she went on with a rueful grin, "all I have to worry about is how I'm ever going to live that little scene down!"

"Don't worry," Susan assured her with a chuckle. "Believe me, Chris, once this is all over and done with, and word gets out about how we helped a talented Russian ballerina defect, I have absolutely no doubt that your behavior will be considered truly heroic by everyone who knows you."

"Do you really think so?"

"Of course! And that's just the beginning of it. Just *think* of all the people who are going to read about this in the newspaper. Why, I bet every single paper in the country will pick up this story."

"Sooz . . ."

"And then there's the radio, don't forget. This is just the kind of thing they love to talk about on those news stations. And then, of course, there's—"

"Don't say it! Not *television*!" Chris groaned loudly.

"Is this really going to turn out to be such a big deal, do you think?"

"Well, of course it will, Chris! I can already see the newspaper headlines." Susan closed her eyes, swept her hand across the air, and said in a dramatic voice, "'Whittington Girl Helps Russian Ballerina Leap to Freedom!' Why, it's guaranteed to be on the front page of every newspaper in the entire country!"

"Very catchy." By this point, even Chris was able to laugh. "But you left out one key fact, my dear sister."

Puzzled, Susan thought for a few seconds. "What could I possibly have left out, Chris?"

"That headline will have to read, 'Whittington *Twins* Help Russian Ballerina Leap to Freedom!' After all, you and I are in this together, right? And you deserve half the credit!"

Chris and Susan spent a few moments basking in the delicious fantasy of all the glory they would receive after this daring escapade that still lay ahead of them had been completed. But then, all of a sudden, Susan grew very serious.

"Wait a minute, Chris. This may all be well and good, talking about what big celebrities you and I are going to be once this whole thing has been carried out—one hundred percent successfully, of course. But in the meantime, there's still one minor detail to be worked out."

Now it was Chris's turn to be puzzled. "What's that, Sooz?"

"We have yet to figure out what this little plan of ours *is!* We still haven't come up with a way to help Natasha get away from those two busybody chaperones who are always following her around!"

"Oh, yeah; I almost forgot." Chris immediately grew somber.

The two girls lapsed into thoughtful silence. Both of them were racking their brains, trying to come up with something. But even as they concentrated as hard as they could, they couldn't seem to come up with a single idea.

"Sooz, all of a sudden I'm not so sure about all this." Chris was now sounding morose. "Maybe I shouldn't have gone ahead and told Natasha that we'd help her out when we hadn't even come up with a plan yet."

Susan could see how upset her sister was, and she tried to be encouraging.

"Don't worry, Chris. We'll come up with something. Don't forget; this is only Friday. We still have until tomorrow night—or even Sunday morning, for that matter—to cook up some little scheme. That's two whole days."

"Two days!" Chris groaned loudly. "That doesn't sound like very much time at all."

But Susan refused to become upset. "Nonsense. You and I have come up with fantastic schemes in much shorter amounts of time than that."

"Well . . . I guess you could be right. . . ."

"Of course I'm right! Come on, Chris; have a little confidence in the Pratt twins' abilities as schemers!" Despite her enthusiasm, however, she could see that her pep talk wasn't doing much good. Chris still looked as if she were down in the dumps.

"Here, I'll tell you what. How about if we try thinking about something else for a change? You know, something that'll help us both take our minds off this for a while."

"Okay, Sooz. I guess that's not a bad idea."

At least there was a hint of optimism in Chris's voice

once again. Susan couldn't help feeling just a little bit satisfied.

"Well, let's see." She glanced around the hotel room, hoping to find something that would hold her twin's attention for a while—at least until she snapped out of this discouraged mood of hers. "Oh, I know!" Susan had just spotted the shopping bag from that morning's buying spree in Georgetown. It was tucked away in a corner, next to the dresser, and she had forgotten all about it. "Why don't you try on the new dress I bought you today?"

"Oh, that's a great idea! Why, I can't wait to see how I look in it. Why don't you try on yours, too?"

"Okay." Susan had already tried hers on, back at the store. But if it would help Chris cheer up, she was willing to put it on again.

Chattering away about all the places they could wear their new dresses, Chris and Susan took them out of the bag and slipped them on. Not surprisingly, once they did, the two girls looked exactly the same. The twins stood in front of the mirror, looking at their reflection.

"Oh, it's such a cute dress!" Chris exclaimed. "I really like the way it fits. And I *love* the color. This shade of pink is gorgeous."

"It's the color of pink lemonade!" Susan reminded her with a chuckle. "I must say, I think the salesclerk thought that Beth and I were going a little bit overboard. I mean, there we were, standing at the counter together, and she was buying one of these dresses, and I was buying *two*. . . . Chris, are you listening to me?"

Even as she spoke to her twin, Susan couldn't help noticing that Chris suddenly had that peculiar, faraway look in her eyes, the look that said she wasn't really listening at all.

"Chris, Chris . . . Oh, dear, now what? Have you decided that you don't like the dress, after all?"

"I've got it," Chris whispered, her eyes still glued to the mirror. "I've finally come up with our plan. Sooz, I know how we can help Natasha Samchenko defect!"

"How? What's the plan? Ooh, Chris, I'm so excited I can hardly wait for you to tell me."

"It's so simple that it's—it's ingenius!" Chris's dark brown eyes were glowing as she ran her inspired idea over and over again in her mind.

Susan, meanwhile, was growing so impatient that she was certain she would scream if Chris didn't hurry up and tell her what she was thinking. "Christine . . ."

"Look, Susan. We have three identical dresses in our possession, right?"

"Well, more or less. We do if we can manage to borrow Beth's."

"No problem. We'll just have to come up with a creative reason why we want it. I only hope she's not planning to wear it to the party and the ballet tomorrow evening." Chris's forehead was wrinkled with worry.

Susan was getting impatient once again. "Chris, she brought that green dress of hers to wear Saturday night. You know, the one she wore when Dennis took her out to that fancy French restaurant on her birthday . . . But you still haven't told me the plan!"

"Okay. We've got three identical dresses. We've also got two identical twins . . . and a third person who has the same basic coloring as us, who, with a little planning, could pass for one of us. . . ."

"Christine Pratt! You are driving me up the wall!"

Totally exasperated by this point, Susan threw her hands up into the air. "Will you please stop teasing me with these little clues of yours and just tell me, once and for all, how on earth we're going to help Natasha?"

"All right, here it is." Chris leaned forward, wearing a big grin that made it clear how proud she was. "This Saturday, the night of the party and the dance, you and I are going to show up looking like each other's mirror image. As a matter of fact, we'll both be wearing our new 'pink lemonade' dresses."

"Wait a minute. You mean you *want* Mr. Pirov and Mrs. Korsky to know there are two of us?"

"I sure do!" Chris was growing even more excited as she went on. "Meanwhile, we'll have snuck the *third* pink dress over to Natasha. Let's see . . . maybe one of us could do it at the party."

"I don't know, Chris," Susan interjected nervously. "That may be cutting things a little close, don't you think?"

"Hmmm. Maybe you're right. Well, then, I'll just have to get the pink dress to Natasha *before* Saturday night, to make sure everything proceeds on schedule."

"Good idea, Chris. There's only one small detail you seem to have left out."

"What's that?" Chris looked puzzled.

"You *still* haven't told me what the plan is!"

"Oh, right. Here goes, then. By the end of the performance, you and I will be wearing pink T-shirt dresses, and Natasha will be waiting backstage, having secretly changed into *her* pink dress. She can—oh, I don't know, maybe throw a raincoat over it or something. Anyway, after the performance, you and I will go backstage, supposedly to congratulate Natasha and say good-bye . . . and that's when we'll do it!"

"Do *what*?"

Chris's eyes were big and round. When she spoke, her voice was so soft that it was almost a whisper. "Sooz, I'll *switch places* with Natasha! Then, once she's masquerading as me, she can sneak out of the Kennedy Center with you. As soon as she's away from the chaperones, she can go to the nearest police station and say she wants to defect because she wants artistic freedom!"

Susan gasped. "That *is* inspired, Chris!" But already her mind was racing, becoming clouded with doubts and fears. "But what about *you*, Chris? What happens when Mr. Pirov realizes what you've done . . . and he's got you in his clutches?"

"Oh, come on, Sooz. What could he possibly do to me? After all, I'm an American citizen, so he has no power over me. Besides, I won't have necessarily done anything wrong. All I'll be doing—*if* he even finds me—is sitting in Natasha's dressing room, wearing a pink dress and minding my own business." She sat back and folded her arms across her chest. "So there it is. What do you think?"

Susan eyed her twin warily. "I think you're very brave, Chris."

"Yes, but do you think it'll work?"

"If you don't lose your nerve, it could very well work," Susan replied seriously.

"Well, I'm not the only one who's going to need her nerve," Chris pointed out. "Don't forget, you're playing a big part in this, too."

Susan gulped. "Gee, I almost forgot. I guess I'll have to pull out all the stops on my acting ability, too."

"So, Sooz, are you up for this?"

"I sure am. As a matter of fact, while you've been telling me all this, I even managed to come up with a name for this little caper of ours."

"Really? What is it?"

"Well, Natasha is going to be pretending to be you—and vice versa, right? As if the two of you were carrying out some sort of charade?"

"Right . . ."

"And all three of us will be wearing dresses that are the color of pink lemonade."

Chris burst out laughing. "I think I know what you're about to say, Sooz! Don't tell me!"

In unison, the twins cried out, "The Pink Lemonade Charade!" And then they both broke into hysterical giggling.

Somehow, having something else to think about besides the possible dangers of what they were planning to do—in only twenty-four hours, no less—helped them get over some of their growing nervousness. It even helped them forget, at least for a moment, that the adventure that they were about to embark upon was in an entirely different league from anything else they had ever attempted before.

Nine

The butterflies that were already jumping around inside Chris's stomach as she woke up told her that this was an important day even before she had a chance to remember exactly what day it was. And as soon as she realized that it was already Saturday, the day of the Pink Lemonade Charade, the butterflies went berserk.

There were several things Chris had to accomplish today. First, she had to get Beth to lend her the third pink dress. Fortunately, she and her twin had already devised a way to do that, late the night before. Second, she had to get the dress to Natasha, as well as explain what the Pink Lemonade Charade was all about, without having anyone suspect, especially Mr. Pirov and Mrs. Korsky, whose jobs were to keep an eye out for exactly this type of thing. Third, there was the Pink Lemonade Charade itself, scheduled for that very evening. . . .

I won't think about it right now, Chris thought as she climbed out of bed. I'll just take things one at a time.

That way, she reasoned, she was less likely to become overwhelmed by what she and her sister were trying to do.

When she waltzed into the hotel coffee shop twenty minutes later, wearing her pink dress and looking as cool as if she didn't have a care in the world, she found that Susan was already sitting with Holly and Beth, chatting away as she and her friends ate their breakfast.

So far, so good, thought Chris, forcing herself to smile as she joined the threesome at their table.

"Hi, everybody," she said brightly. "Like my new dress?"

"Well, I certainly do," Beth joked. "I must say, Chris, you have wonderful taste in clothes."

"I'll second that," Susan agreed heartily. "That is definitely a fantastic dress."

Holly looked up from her waffles with surprise. "What's all this? I mean, the dress is cute, but you're all acting as if it were a designer original or something."

The others laughed, and then explained how all three of them happened to own the same dress.

"Yes, I couldn't wait to wear it," Chris went on to say after she had ordered her scrambled eggs and toast, making sure to tell the waiter she wanted lots of grape jelly with her order. "Sure, I plan to wear it tonight, to the party and the ballet performance. And maybe I should have waited. But you know me; once I get something new, I can't wait to put it on!"

"Just be careful you don't get it dirty," Susan made a point of warning her.

"Oh, come on, Susan," Holly protested. "Chris is a big girl. She can manage to go a whole day without getting her clothes stained!"

Susan and Chris just exchanged amused glances.

"So, Beth, what have you got lined up for today?" Holly asked as the waiter placed Chris's breakfast on the table and she dug right into it.

"Actually, I thought I'd go to the zoo," Beth replied. "The National Zoo is supposed to be one of the finest in the country."

"What a great idea!" Susan exclaimed. "That's where the pandas are! Ooh, I think I'll go, too." Without thinking, she turned to her sister. "How about you, Chris? Care to join us?"

"Oh, gee, Sooz, I don't know. . . ."

"Oh, come on, Chris. Why not?"

Susan froze the moment she realized "why not." But it was already too late; both Beth and Holly were looking at Chris expectantly.

Fortunately, Chris had always been good at thinking on her feet. "As a matter of fact, there is something I want to do this morning, but it's a secret."

"A secret!" That, of course, made Holly and Beth more curious than ever.

"If Chris wants to keep it a secret," Susan insisted, "we should respect that. After all, a girl's entitled to her privacy." The look she gave her sister, however, showed that she was utterly confused by Chris's reply to her question.

"Well, there is one thing I can tell you . . . no, two."

This time, the look that Susan cast her twin was one of shock.

"Okay, Chris," Holly said cheerfully, unaware of all the tension between the twin sisters during this seemingly innocent conversation. "Give us some clues."

"All right. One is that you'll find out tomorrow what this morning's 'secret' was all about. And the other is that . . . well, what I plan to do today has a lot to do with a decision I've made about my future."

"My, my. That certainly sounds serious," Beth observed.

Susan just looked puzzled. Sure, she understood what Chris was referring to by her first "clue." Of course, by tomorrow everyone would know what Chris had been up to. As far as the second part, however, she was totally in the dark. And here she had always prided herself on knowing her twin sister so well!

Chris, meanwhile, glanced over at her best friend. "Holly knows what I'm talking about. Don't you, Holly?"

"Well, sure, but . . . Well, in that case, I can hardly wait! It sounds like Chris here has finally decided what she wants to be when she grows up," she added with a teasing grin.

Susan just continued to look baffled.

"Well," Holly went on, tucking some dollar bills under her plate and slinging her pocketbook over her shoulder, "what do you say the rest of us—those of us with boring, unmysterious lives—start heading for the zoo?"

Susan cast her twin a meaningful glance. But Chris didn't need to be reminded that for Phase One of the Pink Lemonade Charade, it was now or never.

"Sounds like a good idea. Have fun!" Chris said loudly.

Just then, she scooped up a huge glob of purple grape jelly with a knife, went to smear it on top of a piece of toast, and promptly dropped it smack in the middle of her lap instead.

"My dress!" she cried, standing up quickly so that the jelly dribbled down across the skirt, making what would have been only a small stain into a huge one. "I've ruined it! It's *purple*!"

Immediately the three other girls grabbed their napkins and starting dabbing at the stain. But their attempts at banishing the purple blobs on the bright pink fabric proved futile.

"You'd better take that dress upstairs and soak it in cold water right away," Susan told her while Beth and Holly looked on sorrowfully.

"Good idea," Holly agreed. "Before it has a chance to set in."

"But I really wanted to wear this dress today!" Chris wailed.

"Don't worry," her sister said. "If you rinse it out now, it'll be dry by tonight."

"But you don't understand!" Chris insisted. "I wanted to wear it today!" She pretended that she had just gotten a brainstorm. "Hey, Susan, how about if you let me borrow *your* pink dress today? I'm dying to wear something new, you know. I mean, this is practically my last day in Washington, and I just feel like looking really nice. . . ."

"No way!" Susan cried. "Not when you're such a butterfingers!"

"Oh, come on. Don't be such a spoilsport." By now, Chris was pretending to be very upset. "Please! It'd mean so much to me. . . ."

"You can borrow my pink dress," Beth suddenly offered, her voice so soft that Chris might not even have heard her if she hadn't had her ears on the alert for that very invitation.

"Really?" Chris blinked. "You mean you'd really let me borrow your dress today? Oh, I promise I'll be careful, Beth. I—I won't eat a single thing all day. I'll do anything to keep it from getting ruined, now that I've seen what a klutz I can be."

"You don't have to starve yourself," Beth said with a chuckle. "You can borrow it, Chris, if it means that much to you."

"Oh, boy! Thanks a million, Beth. You won't be sorry; I promise." Chris couldn't resist casting a meaningful glance in her twin's direction.

Immediately after breakfast, Chris hurried back to her room and rinsed out her pink dress. Much to her relief, she discovered that the purple stains came right out. She hung it up in front of an open window; that way, it was sure to be dry by that evening. Then she took the key that Beth had lent her, retrieved the third pink dress from the room that Beth and Susan were sharing, and tucked it into a plastic bag.

While she was proceeding with speed and confidence, the truth of the matter was that Chris had yet to figure out how on earth she was going to get to Natasha during the Russian ballet troupe's Saturday morning rehearsal. But then, as she was about to leave Beth and Susan's room and she returned to the closet to put back the empty hanger on which Beth's pink dress had been hung, she had an inspiration.

Less than an hour later, Chris was striding into the main entrance of the rehearsal hall, dressed in one of her twin's most serious-looking outfits: a white blouse, a dark skirt, and simple low-heeled shoes. Under her arm she was carrying a notebook, one she'd picked up at the stationery store she'd found right around the corner from the hotel. When the receptionist right inside the front door glanced up, Chris was ready.

"Good morning. My name is Mary McGregor, and I'm here to interview some of the Russian dancers for my high school English project."

The receptionist just looked bored. "Do you have an appointment?"

"I certainly do. As a matter of fact, if I don't scoot inside right away, I'm going to be late. And if I don't get this term paper written, my English teacher is going to flunk me."

Fortunately, her plea worked. The receptionist's expression went from bored to sympathetic. "Go right in," she said.

Once inside, Chris hurried directly to the one place she knew she had at least a chance of getting Natasha alone—and the one place the chaperones probably wouldn't bother to accompany the dancers. There was a women's rest room right outside the rehearsal hall. Before she ducked inside, prepared to wait as long as she had to, she glanced through the glass door to the large dance studio and saw that the dancer's were already gathering, stretching, and warming up for the workout ahead.

Luckily, she didn't have to wait very long. Before she had been waiting for more than ten minutes, she heard the doorknob start to turn. She hid inside one of the booths and locked the door, which enabled her to see who had come in without being seen herself, and without anyone becoming suspicious.

From her hiding place, Chris saw right away that it

was Natasha who had come in, wearing a leotard and carrying a large tote bag over her shoulder. The pretty dancer looked into the mirror, scowled, and muttered something in Russian. Then she took out a comb and proceeded to fuss with her dark hair, pulled back into a tight bun; that is, except for single strand that kept popping out.

"Natasha!" Chris whispered, stepping out so that her friend could see her.

"Christine! What are you doing here?"

"Sh-h-h. We don't have much time." Chris handed her the bundle she had brought along. "Quick, put this in your bag. It's a dress. Wear it tonight after the performance, but don't let anyone know you've got it on."

Natasha nodded. "I will wear bathrobe over it."

"Good. And make sure you're wearing your hair the same way it is now. Then just wait for us in your dressing room. Susan and I will come as soon as we can, pretending to congratulate you and say good-bye. But when no one is looking, you and I will switch places. You and Susan will leave together, as two twins, both wearing pink dresses, the same way we came in. Meanwhile, I'll stay in your dressing room for a while, then leave a few minutes later. Okay?"

Chris looked at Natasha, half expecting her to laugh at the plan, or burst into tears, or, worse yet, act as if she had no idea what Chris was talking about. Instead, she tucked the dress into her tote bag. Then she grabbed Chris's hand.

"Is good plan," she whispered. The look in her dark brown eyes showed exactly how grateful she was.

And then the moment had passed. From outside in the hall came the sound of two girls chattering gaily in

Russian. Natasha turned back to the mirror, her expression growing stern as she returned to fixing her hair. Chris, meanwhile, ducked back into one of the booths, locking the door.

From her vantage point, she watched while the three Russian dancers fussed with their hair and talked. It was obvious that all three of them were nervous and excited about tonight.

The dancers may be nervous about tonight, Chris thought ruefully as she slipped unseen out of the washroom after the dancers had left and the piano music she heard from the studio told her that the rehearsal was now under way. But not nearly as nervous as some of the members of their audience are!

Ten

"*Well, Chris, I guess this is it.*" *Susan took a deep* breath, then looked over at her sister's reflection in the mirror. "Are you ready for the Pink Lemonade Charade to begin?"

The Pratt twins were standing in front of the full-length mirror on the back of the door in the hotel room that Chris and Holly were sharing. Holly had left long before; she was attending a short preperformance lecture, given by one of the Russian dancers, on *Coppelia*, the ballet the Whittington High School students would be seeing later on that night.

Chris and Susan, however, had passed on the lecture. As much as they would have liked to have heard it, they had much more important things to do early this evening, before the party the American students were holding in honor of the ballet dancers, before the Russian dance troupe's gala performance, and, of course, before the final moments of the Pink Lemonade Charade.

One of the things they had to do, probably the most important, was prepare themselves. They needed time to calm their jitters, and to make sure that every single detail had been carefully thought through. After all, this escapade that was about to get under way was easily the riskiest adventure they had ever undertaken.

And tonight, it was not only themselves who were involved. As they were only too well aware, Natasha Samchenko's entire future rested in their hands.

"Well," Chris said, biting her lip, "I guess I'm as ready as I'll ever be. How do we look?"

Susan studied the reflection in the mirror with a practiced eye. What she saw was two girls who, even to her, looked identical. They had both pulled their dark chestnut brown hair back into low ponytails at the base of their necks. They had made a point of not wearing any jewelry at all, not even wristwatches or earrings, and their makeup was simple. And, of course, they were both wearing the same dresses, the new T-shirt dresses that were the color of pink lemonade.

"'How do we look?' We look like twins," Susan replied with a nervous laugh.

"Good," Chris replied with a chuckle, glancing at her sister. "And just think: In a few more hours, we're going to look like *triplets*."

By the time the girls went inside the elegant hotel in which the Russian dancers were staying, much of their nervousness had vanished. Now that it was time for the party at which the Whittington High School students were playing host to their visitors, they were as excited as they would be on their way to any other party.

This one, in particular, promised to be fun, one of the highlights of their trip. It was being held in one of the meeting rooms on the mezzanine of the hotel, where there would be lots of loud rock music, a buffet of both Russian delicacies and American favorites like hot dogs, Rocky Road ice cream, and even pink lemonade, and, most important, the first real opportunity for the American high school students to get to know the Russian dancers.

"Gee, this looks as if it's really going to be some party, doesn't it?" Susan commented as the twins rounded a corner and found themselves standing in the doorway of the meeting room in which the festivities were already well under way.

There were balloons hanging from the ceiling and crepe-paper streamers everywhere, all in pastel shades of pink, yellow, blue, and green, just perfect for spring. There was, indeed, loud music; the number one hit in the country was blasting from the stereo at full volume, and a few couples had ventured out into the area designated as the dance floor.

Everyone was dressed up, looking their best. And it was apparent that both the Americans and the Russians were committed to meeting each other, overcoming whatever shyness they may have been experiencing in order to take advantage of this unique opportunity, talking and laughing and becoming friends.

Despite all this activity, however, the Pratt twins' entrance caused quite a sensation.

"There are *two* of you!" sputtered Mr. Pirov as soon as he saw the twins come into the room. He started over in their direction. Mrs. Korsky, the girls noticed, followed close behind, and the look on her face made it clear that she was just as astonished as her fellow "chaperone."

Susan and Chris just looked at each other and grinned.

The first thing they did was head for the refreshments, where a huge glass punch bowl was filled with pink lemonade. As they helped themselves, they tried to ignore the two Russian chaperones, but they were well aware that their eyes were glued to these two girls who looked like mirror images of each other.

"So far, so good," Chris whispered to Susan as she leaned across the buffet table to grab a paper napkin.

Susan just smiled.

"Christine, you have made—how you say—'big splash!'" Chris heard someone say, in a gleeful voice. She turned around and grinned at Natasha.

"That's how Susan and I like to do things," she replied with a chuckle. "When we decide to do something, we always do it right. By the way, Natasha, I don't believe you've actually had a chance to meet my twin sister—my *identical* twin sister. Natasha, this is Susan Pratt. Sooz, Natasha Samchenko."

"I am very happy to make your acquaintance, Susan Pratt," Natasha said earnestly. And the look in her dark eyes as she shook Susan's hand made it clear just how true that statement was.

"Now," Natasha said brightly, "is time for you to meet my friends. Katya, Ivan, Dimitri, come meet my two American—what is word I look for—'buddies?'"

For the next hours, Chris and Susan had more fun than they could remember having had in a very long time. Natasha introduced them to every one of the dancers, all of whom were interested in finding out more about these two girls who looked so much the same. The twins danced with practically every boy in the Russian troupe. They were both amazed to discover how easy it was to have a good time with these new friends of theirs. It hardly mattered at all that their two languages were so different, and that some of the dancers knew very little English.

"Gee, Sooz, I sure wish I'd brushed up on my Russian before this trip," Chris joked over her shoulder as she danced with Ivan and Susan twirled around with Dimitri. "I could have at least learned how to ask a few questions, like 'How do you like the United States so far?' "

"The only problem would have been that you wouldn't have been able to understand anyone's answer!" Susan replied, laughing.

The Russian boys weren't the only ones that the twins danced with. Gary and Tim both insisted on claiming one of the dances as theirs, and Chris and Susan gladly took a break from their "cultural exchange" for a few minutes in order to reestablish their ties with these boys from their own country.

It seemed like the perfect get-together—that is, until Skip Desmond joined the party, making a boisterous entrance that called attention to the fact that he was the only one who hadn't been able to show up on time this evening.

He swaggered in, looking as if he were heading for trouble even before he'd had a chance to say a word to anyone. Susan noticed that the teachers from their school, Ms. Parker and some of the others who were acting as chaperones this evening, looked a bit uncomfortable as he came in. Even Mr. Pirov and Mrs. Korsky seemed to take notice of his arrival.

Skip made a point of popping one of the balloons so that everyone in the place jumped. He snickered when everyone looked up to see what had made the loud noise.

"Hey, everybody, how's it going?" he asked casually.

He glared at the Russian dancers, and then headed for the refreshments, pushing his way through the crowd so roughly that he spilled a cup of pink lemonade all over Beth's pretty green dress. Immediately Holly rushed over and began wiping at the stain with paper napkins.

"This is starting to get out of hand," Susan whispered to Chris. "I have a feeling that somebody had better put a stop to Skip's shenanigans before he makes some *real* trouble."

But before Chris had had a chance to reply, Skip noticed the Pratt twins, standing together at the other side of the room, watching his every move and frowning with disapproval. As soon as he saw them, he abandoned the refreshment table and headed in their direction.

"Uh-oh," Chris breathed. "At the risk of sounding trite, here comes trouble."

"Don't worry," Susan assured her. "There are so many people around, he wouldn't dare do anything too terrible." She only wished she were as confident about her statement as she had managed to sound.

"Well, well, well, if it isn't my favorite little snob," Skip said loudly, looking at Chris with a frightening coldness in his eyes.

"Hello, Skip," Chris returned coolly. "Glad you could make it tonight," she added sarcastically.

"Oh, yeah?" Skip's tone had already softened. Pretending to misunderstand her comment, he came over and put his arm around her waist. "See, I've been trying to tell you for a while now that you and I were made for each other. I'm glad I'm finally starting to get to you."

"Oh, you're definitely getting to me, but not in the way you mean." Firmly Chris removed his hand from her waist, stepping aside so that she was no longer within his easy reach.

"Well, then, I guess I'll just have to start putting more energy into changing your mind about that." He folded his arms across his chest and looked at Susan. "Now how about if you disappear, Sis? Your twin and I have some things to discuss."

"Susan isn't going anywhere," Chris said firmly.

"Oh, yeah? What, you need a chaperone?"

"With you around, I think what I need is a *body-guard.*"

Skip just laughed.

By that time, several people had noticed the unpleasant interchange going on in the corner of the room. Even Mr. Pirov and Mrs. Korsky were looking on nervously.

And then Ivan, the Russian dancer who was one of Natasha's friends, sauntered over, keeping a friendly look on his face even though it was obvious by his actions that he was concerned.

"Hello, Christine," he said. "Would you like to dance?"

"Flake off, pal," Skip returned belligerently. "Chris here has just promised to dance every dance for the rest of the night with me. Besides, shouldn't you be polishing your toe shoes or something?"

"I'd be careful if I were you, Skip," Susan interjected. "Ivan here is a lot bigger than you. Stronger, too, as you can see for yourself—that is, if you're not too busy making a fool of yourself to check out the muscles on his arms."

"Huh! I'm not afraid of any foreigner. Especially some guy who can hardly speak English."

Suddenly Skip seemed to realize that it didn't make sense to push Ivan too far. He turned his attention back to Chris.

"Come on, sweets. It's time for you and me to show this guy what dancing is *really* all about."

He grabbed Chris by the wrist and pulled her out onto the dance floor, using such force that she nearly lost her balance.

"*Stop* it!" she cried, trying to break away from his insistent grasp. "Leave me alone, Skip. You're really going too far."

"Hey, come on. Don't be such a party pooper. I thought you were a girl who likes to have a good time."

"Not with someone like you!" Once again, Chris tried to get away from him, but he still held onto her arm.

"Relax, Chris. I'm telling you, you and I could make quite a pair, if you'd just give me a chance."

"Skip, cut it out." She looked around for Ms. Parker, but the chaperone was nowhere to be seen.

Despite her protests, however, Chris knew that nothing she could say would make any difference to this boy. She glanced over at Ivan, and saw from the angry look in his eyes that he was about to forget his manners and take the matter into his own hands in about another thirty seconds. And a fight was the last thing Chris wanted.

All of a sudden, without even thinking, she reached over toward the buffet table and grabbed a half-drunk cup of pink lemonade that someone had left there. And just as impetuously, she dumped it all over Skip's head.

"What . . . how! . . ." he sputtered, blinking and swiping at his eyes as the cold pink liquid dripped off his hair, all over his face, and onto his clothes. When he finally managed to open his eyes, Chris was surprised to see that he looked more hurt than angry.

"What did you do *that* for?" he demanded.

"I'm sorry, Skip, but you didn't seem to believe me when I told you I had no interest in dancing with you," Chris replied coldly. "So I had to resort to some other way of letting you know how serious I was."

"Why, you little! . . ."

But Chris didn't wait around to hear what else he had to say. She stalked away, so angry and upset that she was actually shaking. She was aware that everyone in the room was looking at her, and at Skip, standing in the middle of the room, sopping wet and still sputtering incoherently.

Fortunately, another record came on just then, and Holly made a point of dragging Hank onto the dance floor. Katya and Dimitri followed, then Natasha and Ivan, and it wasn't long before the party was under way once again.

By the time Chris had the nerve to glance over at Skip, he was gone, having rushed out of the room as quickly as he could.

"Gee, Chris, are you all right?" Susan asked once her twin had joined her in the corner of the room once again.

"Yes, I'm fine." Chris bit her lip, then suddenly broke into a huge grin. "Skip sure looked surprised when I poured that pink lemonade all over his head, didn't he?"

"I'll say." Instead of smiling, however, Susan just looked worried. "Oh, Chris, of course you were right to stand up for yourself, and he certainly deserved what he got . . . but what do you think will happen now?"

"Who cares? He's gone, isn't he? The party can go on,

and everyone can keep having a good time—just as they were *before* that troublemaker showed up here."

"I guess so," Susan replied.

She forced a smile, having decided to keep her fears to herself.

Skip Desmond is the kind of boy who won't take an affront like that lying down, she was thinking. Now that Chris insulted him, and in front of so many people, too, I wouldn't be at all surprised if he decided to seek some kind of revenge.

Oh, dear, she thought, her forehead furrowed with worry even as she accepted Tim's invitation for another dance, if he does decide to get back at Chris, I sure hope he doesn't try anything tonight! The *last* thing we need is for Skip Desmond to do something that might get in the way of the Pink Lemonade Charade!

Eleven

The Russian ballet troupe's performance of Coppelia was exquisite. Susan and Chris sat on the edge of their seats in one of the three theaters comprising the Kennedy Center. It was elegant and understated with its comfortable upholstered seats and its thick carpets in a deep, rich red. Their eyes remained glued to the stage for almost two hours, as if they had been hypnotized. Before them unfolded a romantic story about a beautiful doll who came to life, with Natasha Samchenko dancing the lead role.

"Gee, this has got to be the most wonderful performance I've ever seen in my entire life," Susan whispered to her twin sister as the audience around them applauded a particularly lovely dance that Natasha had just done. Every one of her movements had been perfect, and on the stage, she looked even more graceful than she had during rehearsals.

"I'll say!" Chris agreed heartily, whispering back.

"Natasha is even better than I ever dreamed. And the costumes are sensational, the scenery is great, the orchestra is wonderful. . . . I like ballet more than I ever would have thought."

The twins were indeed enjoying the ballet. Even so, neither one of them could completely ignore the fear that tugged at them throughout, not letting them forget, even for a moment, that something much more important than the memorable performance of *Coppelia* still lay ahead of them this evening.

"Goodness, that was really something!" Susan said once the ballet was over, making certain that her comment would be overheard by at least some of her classmates.

The applause had ended, four curtain calls had been taken, and Natasha had modestly accepted a bouquet of two dozen red roses with tears in her eyes. Now the members of the audience were standing up to leave, folding up their programs and gathering up jackets and pocketbooks as they prepared to leave the Kennedy Center.

Susan and Chris, of course, had no intention of leaving. At least, not yet.

"Yes, it was really something." Chris made a point of agreeing with her sister in an equally loud voice. "Hey, Sooz, I just had a brainstorm. What do you say you and I go backstage and congratulate Natasha on her outstanding performance? I'm sure she'd want to hear about how much we enjoyed the entire ballet."

"That's a wonderful idea!" Susan replied enthusiastically. "Besides, that'll give us a chance to say good-bye to Natasha. Don't forget, we're going back home tomorrow, and so is she. This will be our last chance to see her."

The two girls, dressed in identical pink dresses and wearing their hair in the same style, made their way backstage.

Not surprisingly, there was a flurry of excitement behind the scenes. The ballet dancers were excited about the success of their performance, and more than a little bit relieved. They stood in the wings, talking and laughing and congratulating each other. It was fun, seeing them all in their costumes and their elaborate makeup, relaxing amidst the lights and ropes and cables and scenery that were all tucked away backstage. But as much as Susan and Chris would have loved to linger, they moved through the crowd with determination.

"Hello, Susan! Hello, Christine!" the girls' new Russian friends called to them as they passed through the throng of dancers.

"Hi, everybody!" Chris returned.

"We loved the ballet," said Susan. "It was magnificent!"

"Thank you," said Dimitri. "Where are you girls going now?"

"Oh, just to see Natasha," Chris replied casually.

"That's right," Susan agreed. "We want to congratulate her on her performance, and say good-bye."

Mr. Pirov and Mrs. Korsky, the twins noticed, were lurking on the sidelines, listening to every word that was said. The girls made their way quickly through the wings, more aware than ever of how important—and how dangerous—their mission really was.

They found a corridor behind the stage, off of which

the dressing rooms were located. It didn't take long for them to find the one that was Natasha's.

Just as the twins had expected, they found her alone, waiting for them.

"Natasha! Here you are!" Chris said loudly as she burst into the dressing room. As far as she was concerned, she wanted to make everything she and her sister did and said seem as natural as possible. After all, she was only too aware that it was impossible to know exactly who might be taking note of their actions.

"We *loved* the ballet," Susan added, sounding just as dramatic. "And you were wonderful. Watching you dance was quite an experience. Tonight's a night I'll never forget."

"Me, either!" her twin agreed.

Natasha, meanwhile, was sitting on a small couch in the dressing room, looking so calm that the twins both found themselves wondering if perhaps she had changed her mind about going through with the Pink Lemonade Charade. But then, from underneath the blue bathrobe she was wearing, a small piece of pink fabric slipped out at the hem. Quickly Natasha tucked it away, but not before giving Chris and Susan a look that told them she was more than ready to proceed.

"Thank you so much, Susan and Christine. I am pleased you have enjoyed the ballet so much."

"We sure did. It was great." As Chris spoke, she gently shut the door behind her. Even so, the three girls continued with their little charade, acting as if the Pratt twins were, indeed, up to nothing more than a friendly backstage visit with their new friend and favorite ballerina.

But once the door was closed, Natasha stood up, slipped off her bathrobe, and hung it on a hook.

"I hope you were able to follow the story," Natasha said. "Is such a lovely story, all about little doll who comes to life."

"Oh, yes!" Chris said heartily. "We could tell exactly what was going on."

After casting a rueful look at her twin, she exchanged places with Natasha, taking the seat on the couch where only moments before the Russian girl had been sitting. Natasha, meanwhile, now stood where Chris had been, right next to Susan.

Chris surveyed them both nervously.

Yes, she decided, if no one looks at their faces *too* closely, Natasha just might manage to pass herself off as Christine Pratt. . . .

"Well," Susan said, suddenly anxious to get away, "we'd better not take up any more of your time, Natasha. We just wanted to say good-bye. We both really enjoyed getting to know you."

"Good-bye, good-bye!" all three girls called loudly.

And then, without wasting another moment, Susan and Natasha left the dressing room, closing the door behind them.

They walked quickly, but not as if they were in a hurry. Natasha took care to keep her head down, and to try to stay in the shadows as she walked. Susan, meanwhile, chattered away, acting as if absolutely nothing were out of the ordinary.

"Gee, that was such a wonderful ballet," she said loudly. "And that Natasha certainly is nice. She's an incredible dancer, too."

"Mmph," Natasha mumbled, nodding.

"I, um, wonder if, um, we'll ever get to see her again." In her growing nervousness, Susan was running out of things to say. But she forced herself to keep talking as the two girls continued to walk down the corridor, through the Kennedy Center's backstage area, heading toward the back doors. "Maybe we could keep in touch. You know, write letters back and forth."

So far, so good, Susan was thinking.

And then, all of a sudden, her heartbeat quickened. There, up ahead, was a small group of ballet dancers, the other members of the dance troupe that the twins had passed on their way to the dressing room; dancers who would, of course, recognize Natasha immediately.

"Uh-oh," she whispered. "Here comes Ivan and Dimitri and Katya."

Natasha muttered something in Russian. Susan didn't need a translation; she could imagine exactly what the Russian girl must be feeling at that moment. Automatically she reached for her arm, gripping it tightly as if to lead her through the obstacle ahead, or at least to offer her support.

"Look! Is twins again!" Ivan called gaily. "Goodbye, Chris and Susan. Thank you for being such kind hostesses here in your country."

And then, when Natasha and Susan were only ten feet or so away from the small gathering of dancers, Susan's heart felt as if it had stopped. There, standing in the shadows behind them, his arms folded firmly across his chest, was Mr. Pirov.

Chris, meanwhile, was sitting alone in the dressing room, waiting, her heart pounding as fast and as hard as a jackhammer.

All I have to do, she was thinking, is stay out of sight for a few more minutes, keeping my fingers crossed and hoping that Susan and Natasha manage to sneak out of the Kennedy Center without any problem. And then, after enough time has gone by, I'll slip out of here myself. And one thing's for sure: As soon as I see Sooz back at the hotel, I'm going to *insist* that she tell me every single detail about how the "Pratt twins" exit went!

She stayed very still, holding her breath as she listened to Susan and Natasha's footsteps fade away, as well as Susan's cheerful voice, going on and on about how much she had enjoyed the ballet. Chris was wondering exactly how long she should stay there, and, in fact, how she would even be sure of how much time had gone by, since she wasn't wearing a wristwatch, when she heard soft footsteps outside the closed door.

Her heart was pounding harder than ever. One thing she was sure of was that less than a minute had passed since Susan and Natasha had left, not nearly enough time for them to slip out of the building. If there really was someone lurking outside, listening, perhaps, anxious to hear what was going on behind the closed door, she would have to do some pretty fancy footwork to stall for time.

And then, after a few seconds of dead silence, she heard the barely perceptible rattle of the doorknob as someone placed a hand on it very lightly. Before she had even had a chance to brace herself, the door swung open.

The worst thing that could possibly have happened had just happened.

Mrs. Korsky, Mr. Pirov's dour sidekick, was standing three feet away from Chris.

The Russian "chaperone's" very first words verified Chris's initial assumption, that she was bound to be wondering what on earth Christine Pratt was doing, sitting all alone in Natasha Samchenko's dressing room.

"Miss Pratt! What are you doing in Natasha's dressing room?" Mrs. Korsky growled. "And which twin are you?"

"I'm Christine, Mrs. Korsky. And I'm, uh, hiding," she replied, unable to conceal her nervousness.

"Hiding? And from whom—or what—are you hiding?"

Chris's mind raced. Her heart was pounding so hard she wondered if Mrs. Korsky could hear it. The only thing she could think of was that she had been caught. And as if that weren't bad enough, she had been caught before Susan and Natasha had had a chance to sneak out of the building, at least according to her mental calculations. If Mrs. Korsky became suspicious and went off in search of her, anxious to find out what was going on, Natasha would be caught . . . and so would Susan. All three of them would be in big trouble. Only the implications for the Russian ballerina would no doubt be far, far greater than they would be for Chris and Susan.

"I . . . uh . . . you . . ."

Chris gulped. Mrs. Korsky was staring at her with cold, hard eyes, her face now only a few inches away from Chris's. Her mind was a blank. She couldn't think straight in this panic she had suddenly been thrown into. . . .

And then, all of a sudden, she had a brainstorm.

"I'm hiding from that awful boy, Skip Desmond." Instantly she had regained her cool. "You've got to help me, Mrs. Korsky. You remember him, don't you?"

"Of course I remember. Everyone at party tonight noticed what a—how do you say, maker of trouble—he was." With a funny little smile, she added, "When you pour drink on him, Christine, I secretly am glad."

Chris couldn't help smiling herself—and not only because she found she was managing successfully to stall for time, either.

See, she thought triumphantly, even Mrs. Korsky has an understanding streak. Maybe, underneath, she's not so bad after all. . . .

But it didn't take long for her to remember what her mission here tonight was all about.

"Yeah, well, that creepy Skip followed me backstage, after the performance—which was beautiful, by the way. We all enjoyed it so much. . . . Anyway, he came after me, still angry about before—not that I blame him, of course, although he only got exactly what he deserved. . . ."

Chris could feel her cheeks growing red as she chattered on and on, trying to hold Mrs. Korsky so that Susan and Natasha would have enough time to get away. But she was terribly frightened, even as she saw that her ploy was actually working. Underneath the fabric of her pink dress, she was trembling all over. And she couldn't help worrying about just how long she could go on.

And then her face lit up as she happened to catch sight of a familiar face passing by in the corridor outside.

"Skip!" she cried, without thinking.

Immediately she clasped her hand over her mouth.

"Uh-oh," she moaned, looking at Mrs. Korsky with what she hoped looked like real terror. "*Now* I've done it! I don't know what came over me. . . ."

"Don't worry," Mrs. Korsky assured her. "I will not let this maker of trouble disturb you any longer."

By then, Skip had realized that it was Chris who had called his name. He came into the dressing room, looking a bit sheepish, she couldn't help noticing.

"Hi, Chris," said Skip, sounding almost friendly. "Beth told me she thought she'd seen you come back here, and I was kind of hoping I'd get a chance to talk to you alone. I wanted to say something about what happened before—"

"Get away from me, you—you animal!" Chris cried, jumping back and pretending to be afraid. "You won't get away with any more of your childish behavior!"

"Yeah, well, I've been meaning to talk to you about that—"

"Don't you touch me!"

"Hey, I didn't come *near* you—"

"Young man," Mrs. Korsky interrupted, "I suggest that you leave right now, before there is any more trouble. You have bothered this nice young woman enough for one night."

"Wait a second. I didn't—"

"Enough!"

Chris didn't know whether she felt like laughing or crying as she watched Skip slink away, out of the dressing room. It was obvious to her that he had come looking for her in order to try to apologize, to set things right between them, once and for all; yet she had been forced to go on pretending they were the worst of enemies.

Still, she had to keep things in perspective. After all, there was something much bigger going on here; she simply had to keep that in mind.

I'll just have to set things right with Skip some other time, she thought ruefully.

As for now, Mrs. Korsky had taken it upon herself to escort Chris back to her group personally, and Chris had every intention of making sure they took a different route to the lobby than the one she knew Susan and Natasha were taking.

"Christine Pratt, I will stay with you until you are back with the others to make sure that no harm comes to you tonight from that—that—" And she finished her sentence by saying a word in Russian.

"Thanks a lot, Mrs. Korsky," said Chris. And despite the terror that still gripped her heart, she smiled.

Meanwhile, Susan was resisting the temptation to break into a run, dragging Natasha along with her, past Dimitri and Ivan and Katya, past Mr. Pirov, out of the Kennedy Center.

I have to act natural, she was thinking.

She glanced over at her Russian friend, expecting that there would be terror in Natasha's eyes. Instead, she was surprised to see that she looked perfectly calm. And then she remember that *acting* was part of dancing ballet.

Even so, she knew that Natasha had to be at least as frightened as she was. After all, even before they reached Mr. Pirov, they had to pass by three of Natasha's good friends. Her "disguise" would only do so much good; they both knew full well that if she were forced to utter even a single word in her attempt to act the part of one of the Pratt twins, her accent would give her away.

Susan decided it was time for a quick switch of personalities.

"Hi, guys!" she said loudly. "Boy oh boy, as sure as

my name is Christine Pratt, I've never been so impressed with anything in my entire life! The way you all performed tonight! . . . Wow, this sure was something I'll never forget!"

"How about you, Susan?" Katya asked politely. The backstage area was in half-darkness by now, since the theater hands were preparing to close up for the night. Natasha was also standing in a deep shadow, keeping her head down and letting her hair fall across her face. Susan could feel her tension as she stood there, with Katya, her closest friend in the whole world, standing only a few feet away. And, of course, she was only too aware that Mr. Pirov was still lurking just a few yards behind the others.

"Oh, you know Sooz," Susan said gaily, forcing a loud laugh. "She *loves* ballet! She thought this was the greatest night of her life! Didn't you, Sooz?"

She turned to Natasha, expecting her to nod. But instead, as she looked over, she saw that Natasha's and Katya's eyes had locked. Natasha's eyes were pleading. The expression on Katya's face, meanwhile, was at first one of recognition, and then one of surprise.

At about the same moment, Ivan and Dimitri also leaned forward and took a closer look at Susan's companion. Their faces registered the same shock.

Susan held her breath.

And then, suddenly, in a low, even voice, Katya said, "Susan and Chris, you had both better hurry back to your group. You do not want to miss the bus back to your hotel."

Then, almost as if it had been prearranged, Katya, Ivan, and Dimitri gathered around the two girls, conversing naturally as they escorted them toward the back doors.

As they were about to pass Mr. Pirov, Ivan broke away from the small group, exclaiming, "Mr. Pirov, I just realized that I don't have my airplane ticket! It is not in my dressing room, and I am certain I did not leave it at the hotel."

"Ivan, you should know that *I* have your ticket." And then Mr. Pirov went on talking to Ivan in Russian. As the other dancers passed by with two young women in pink dresses, he never even gave them a second glance.

Susan and Natasha hurried out the back door of the Kennedy Center, toward the taxi stand where they knew they could quickly get away to the closest police station. There, Natasha could quickly declare her intention to defect, for the purpose of artistic freedom.

As Susan called out one last good-bye over her shoulder, catching a final look at Katya and Dimitri as she headed out the back door with Natasha, she squeezed her Russian friend's arm tightly. There were tears in both girls' eyes as, side by side, they walked out of the Kennedy Center together.

Twelve

RUSSIAN BALLERINA DEFECTS! read the headlines of Sunday morning's *Washington Post*.

Chris and Susan couldn't help feeling satisfied as they sat over their celebratory breakfast at the hotel's coffee shop. Susan read the article aloud while Chris sat back in her chair, too excited to touch her food.

"Well, she made it," Susan said with a smile. "The Pink Lemonade Charade really worked. The fact that it's now front-page news proves it!"

"Read me the part about us again," Chris insisted for the third time.

Her sister was only too happy to oblige.

" 'The dark-haired ballerina claims that she never could have carried it off without the aid of two American girls whom she met while the dance troupe was here in Washington for its premier performance. "I owe everything to my new American friends, Christine and Susan Pratt," said Natasha Samchenko, her brown eyes filling with tears. "Without them, I never would have been able to gain my freedom.'"'

"I think we should be pretty proud of ourselves," Chris said, wearing a huge grin.

"Me, too," Susan agreed. "After all, we helped Natasha get exactly what she wanted."

"That's right. We thought up a brilliant scheme, carried it out to the letter. . . ."

"Don't forget," Susan added with a grin, "we never would have managed without a little help from our friends. Or, should I say, a little help from *Natasha's* friends!"

Chris sighed. "Yes, it was all pretty exciting, wasn't it? As a matter of fact, just thinking about it is making me hungry!" Suddenly she had found her appetite. She was just about to start wolfing down her breakfast when their waiter came over to their table.

"Excuse me, but are you two girls the Pratt twins, by any chance?" he asked.

"We certainly are!" Chris turned to her sister. "See, we're already famous!"

"There's a telephone call for Susan Pratt," their waiter went on to say.

Chris was crestfallen. "Is *that* all. And here I was certain he was going to ask for our autograph, or at least compliment us on our bravery."

"Well, who knows?" Susan countered. "Maybe this phone call is from—I don't know, some television station, or—or the president, or—or—"

"You'd better hurry up and take that call!" Chris cried. "Now I'm dying to know what's so important that somebody went to the trouble of tracking us down!"

While Susan scampered away, Chris turned back to

her breakfast, determined to eat at least a little bit of it before giving up on the notion entirely. But then she felt someone's presence nearby. She glanced up and found Skip Desmond hovering near the table.

"Skip! I've been wanting to talk to you!"

"Yeah, well, I've been wanting to talk to you, too." Skip looked upset as he sat down at the table. "Listen, Chris, about last night . . ."

"Oh, I'm sorry! I know I acted terribly, but I was desperate for a way to stall for time while Susan was helping Natasha sneak away, and—and you were the first excuse I could think of, and then the next thing I knew, there you were, and it seemed like the best way to keep Mr. Pirov from getting suspicious—"

"Whoa, hold on!" Skip was smiling as he held up his hands. "Look, Chris, I realize all that—now. After all, I read the newspapers, too. But to tell you the truth, I felt pretty bad last night, after that little scene. I mean, there I was, trying to apologize for acting so stupid lately . . ."

"I know you were. And that's why I feel so bad that I had to pretend you were giving me a hard time."

"At any rate, it's all over now. That is, I'd like it to be. If you're willing to accept my apology, that is, and give me another chance."

"Of course!" Chris breathed. "You know, Skip, I heard through the grapevine that things at your house haven't been going too smoothly lately," she added in a gentle voice.

"Well, that may be the case, but that's still no excuse for the way I've been acting. Especially around you, Chris. But the truth is, well, I've always thought you were kind of special, and I'm afraid I've never been very good at knowing how to act around girls. . . ."

"That's okay. I know how it is."

"So you're not mad at me?"

"No, not anymore."

"And we can be friends?"

"Sure!"

"Great." Skip looked so relieved, and so happy, that Chris's heart went out to him. "Because lately, I'm afraid I've been making more enemies than friends." He stood up then and said, "Well, I'd better go pack. Our bus leaves for the airport in half an hour. Before you know it, we'll all be back in Whittington again. Back to the same old routine."

"Well, not *quite* the same," Chris said. "After all, you and I will both have new friends now. We'll have each other!"

Chris was still smiling a minute or two later, after Skip had gone upstairs to get ready to leave. But the gentle smile on her lips was nothing compared to the huge grin on Susan's face as she sat down at the table.

"That was Mom on the phone," she reported, looking as if she were ready to burst. "She was calling with some good news."

"So good that it couldn't even wait a few hours until we get home this afternoon?" Chris couldn't imagine what could possibly be so important.

But the look on her sister's face told her that it was important, indeed.

"Mom and Dad got in late last night, after being out all day," Susan went on to say. "And when they opened up yesterday's mail first thing this morning, they found an acceptance letter from the Morgan School of Art! I got in!"

"Oh, Sooz! That's fantastic!" Chris squealed, getting up and hugging her sister. "Congratulations! I'm so happy for you!"

"Hey, hey, what's all this?" asked Beth. She and Holly had just come down to breakfast, wanting to grab a quick bite before leaving for the airport.

"Sooz just got some really good news," Chris told them, beaming.

"You mean international fame isn't *enough*?" Holly teased.

"This is even more meaningful," said Susan. She was blushing slightly as she spoke. "I just heard that I've been accepted at art school, at the Morgan School of Art. I've wanted to go there every since . . . well, ever since I can remember, practically."

"That's wonderful!" Beth cried.

"Congratulations!" said Holly.

After the excitement over Susan's acceptance at art school had died down, Chris said, "While we're talking about our futures, I have some good news, too."

Susan couldn't help being curious. "Really, Chris? What's that?"

"Well, I've finally decided what I want to do when I grow up."

Holly, Beth, and Susan all had their eyes glued to Chris.

"I'm going to be a lawyer."

"Chris!" Holly gasped. "That's perfect! Why, I really think you've stumbled upon a career that's just right for you. After all, you're outgoing, and you get along well with people."

"You're not bad when it comes to thinking on your feet, either," Susan added with a chuckle.

"And maybe being able to act a little bit isn't such a bad skill for a lawyer to have," Chris added, only half teasing.

"But all that's only part of it," she went on more seriously. "I realized during this trip, during this whole episode with Natasha, that I'd really like to spend my life helping people protect their freedom. Being able to come through for Natasha meant so much to me. . . ."

"Well, I think it's a great idea." Susan's dark eyes were glowing, largely because she was so proud of her twin sister.

"Hey, what are you four up to?"

Beth, Holly, and the twins looked up and saw Gary and Tim standing there.

"Plotting any more international intrigues?" Gary joked.

"Not exactly. As a matter of fact," Susan said with a smile, "we've just been plotting our futures."

"Well, we'd better start plotting a way to get on that airport bus on time, or we'll end up staying here in Washington forever," said Tim.

"Oh, I wouldn't mind that," Beth returned dreamily. "This is a wonderful place."

"Yes," Chris agreed, standing up. "It *is* a wonderful place, and I had a fantastic time here in Washington, one that I'll never forget. But now that I know where I'm headed, I'm anxious to get going!"

About the Author

Cynthia Blair grew up on Long Island, earned her B.S. from Bryn Mawr College in Pennsylvania, and went on to get a M.S. in marketing from M.I.T. She worked as a marketing manager for food companies but now has abandoned the corporate life in order to write. She lives on Long Island with her husband, Richard Smith, and their son Jesse.